To Susan,

" Happy Chanukah "

Love
Mom

Hot Chicken Wings

Jyl Lynn Felman

aunt lute books
SAN FRANCISCO

First Edition
10-9-8-7-6-5-4-3-2-1

Aunt Lute Books
P.O. Box 410687
San Francisco, CA 94141

Cover and Text Design: Pam Wilson

Cover Art: Karen Babour

Typesetter: Debra DeBondt

Production: Jayna Brown
            Christine Lymbertos
            Cathy Nestor
            Opal Palmer Adisa
            Kathleen Wilkinson

This is a work of fiction. In no way does it intend to represent any real person, living or dead, or any real incidents.

Printed in USA on acid-free paper

Library of Congress in Publication Data

Felman, Jyl Lynn, 1954–
    Hot chicken wings / by Jyl Lynn Felman. — 1st ed.
        p.   cm.
        ISBN: 1-879960-23-0 (lib. ldg.) : $19.95. — ISBN 1-879960-21-4
    (trade pbk.) : $9.95
        1. Lesbians — Fiction.   2. Women, Jewish — Fiction.   I. Title.
    PS3556.E47255H6   1992
    813'.54 — dc20   92-19610
                                                            CIP

The editor gratefully acknowledges the following presses and publications for their kind permission to reprint the works noted below.

"Her Job," from *Korone Volume Seven*, Womanspace, Inc. (1992).

"Jelly Rolls," from *A Loving Voice*, The Charles Press (1991) 258.

"Hot Chicken Wings," from *Tide Lines*, Gynergy Books (1991) 12.

"Miss Ohio," *Korone Volume Six*, Womanspace, Inc. (1990) 32.

"Voices," *Bridges, 1:4* (Spring, 1990) 35.

"Absence," *Bridges, 1:3* (Fall, 1990) 63.

"Crisis," *Speaking For Myself*, Crossing (1990) 57.

"Hot Chicken Wings," *Speaking For Myself*, Crossing (1990) 140.

"Crisis," *Sinister Wisdom, 27* (Fall 1984) 66.

"Jelly Rolls," *Penumbra, 1:2* (1979) 5.

"Zmira," *Syracuse Review, 1:1* (1975) 4.

O Acknowledgements

There are certain people in my life that I want to thank publicly for their support in completing my first collection of short fiction.

For the blessing of friendship that dares to cross forbidden boundaries over and over again, I appreciate Linda Randall and Shirley Hayden Whitley.

My sister in cutting edge, cultural visioning, art as sacred task and text, I honor Sandra Golvin who insisted that I not ever give up.

In her hunger for the passionate word that dares to name the truth and for the unconditional love she has always given me, I thank Deborah P. Britzman.

Because she has never not believed in my vision; and because we are each other's witness, I cherish Carole L. Johnson.

There are three women in particular, from my *Hadassah* chapter, who have nurtured and sustained me with their one-of-a-kind laughter and soulful tears. Whenever I am on the radio, I carry them in my heart. Thank you Lois Bass, Debbie King, and Roberta Issler.

The following people each deserve special mention in my appreciation of their support:

My co-traveler in the wilderness, Stacey Goren, who encouraged me to keep pushing beyond the silence.

Ana Ruiz, Michele Reich, and Jane Seidenberg: the fiesty, luscious girls that I can always eat chicken with and cry.

Joan Featherman led me through the maze without giving up and Tom Herman applauded my arrival; both knew when to break the rules, thank god.

To Carol Potter and Leslie Lawrence, writers I have known and admired for over eighteen years, and who, each in her unique way, assisted me to reach for my own, individual voice, I offer my continued love and commitment.

To my long-lost brother, Lev Raphael, I treasure the phone lines between us.

To Anne and Howard Irwin, I owe my deepest gratitude for their editorial assistance and loving support. And to G.L., *may her memory be a blessing to us all.*

To Jayna Brown, Lisa Kahaleole Hall and Melissa Levin whose publishing expertise I depended on, thank you.

I would also like to thank Opal Palmer Adisa for her editorial help with "Hot Chicken Wings."

I am especially indebted to my editor, Joan Pinkvoss, for the courage of her vision, the risks she took with me and the many leaps we took together.

My earliest readers were my older sisters Judy and Jan; their critical eyes and delight in my stories remain alive in me today.

Finally, for the wonderous gift of the imagination they sparked in me as a young girl and continued to feed at every opportunity, I thank my beloved parents, Edith and Marvin Felman.

For Janet

The Rebbe of Tsanz was asked by a Chasid:
'What does the Rabbi do before praying?'
'I pray,' was the reply,
'that I may be able to pray properly.'

from *Gates of Prayer*

O

Table of Contents

The Forbidden
Or What Makes Me a Jewish Lesbian Writer

I am sitting at the dinner table with my father Marvin and my mother Edith. My sisters, Judy and Jan, are also sitting with us, although it feels to me as though they are sitting at another table on the other side of the room or possibly another restaurant entirely. When we order, I imagine the table splitting in half; Judy and Jan fall off the left side, their silverware and dishes follow noisily behind. The flower arrangement — a limp pink astromaria and a piece of dead green fern — remains upright in a small plastic vase on the right side of the table where I remain split off from my sisters and connected — temporarily — to my parents.

For their entire meal, my sisters have ordered baby-shrimp cocktails in thick-stemmed parfait dishes, with spiced tomato sauce for dipping and dunking. The rest of us order kosher style — no pork, no shellfish, no milk and meat eaten together. My sisters enjoy their food immensely, commenting on the freshness of the fish, its delightful taste and the low calorie count of shrimp. My father makes no eye contact with my sisters; he refuses to even look at their half of the table as though it contains a highly contagious disease that he will catch in a single glance. Judy and Jan make eye contact with their parfait dishes; they smile lovingly at the chilled baby shrimp tucked inside while my mother stares at me, as if the fact that my sisters ordered *treyf* is all my fault. Actually, it is my father's fault. He made a rule.

He made a rule about what his children could eat, what we couldn't eat and when and where we could eat it. With much fierceness he tried to protect us from the *goyim*. It didn't work. At home, my mother kept a strictly kosher kitchen with separate dishes for milk and meat. Absolutely no pork or shellfish was ever allowed in the house. Before arriving in my mother's sink, our chickens were ritually slaughtered and rabbi-blessed. Sticking out of the *tucas* there were always a few feathers left by the *shochet* — firm proof that his chickens were *glatt* kosher. When we finally did eat out, we were allowed to order whatever we wanted. By then my sisters had developed unnatural cravings for shellfish and my mother felt no hunger whatsoever. And me, I developed an insatiable appetite, which manifests itself today in the form of a Jewish lesbian vegetarian chicken writer.

What makes me a Jewish lesbian writer is the fact that my beloved parents kept kosher, and longed for their progeny to do the same. Keeping kosher means eating only that food which is permitted according to Jewish law and avoiding all else — that which is forbidden, is *treyf.* So it is the very act of eating that makes my stories Jewish. Lurking in the background of every scene I write is a sense of the forbidden. The fact that my characters behave in ways that are politically incorrect and that my subject matter is often taboo in both the Jewish and lesbian universe can be traced back to my sisters' unnatural cravings for shellfish. But what makes my stories lesbian with the emphasis on Jewish is the fact that my characters don't just imagine what eating pussy is like, they actually eat it. And eating pussy for me is just like eating *treyf.*

Culturally specific metaphors compel the direction of my narrative voice. For instance, I am preoccupied with otherness not just because I am a lesbian, but because I am a Jew. My characters are obsessed with identity in general, not just gay or Jewish identity. Voice for me is oral, not linear. Sentences that feel flat on the page, live when spoken. I come from an oral tradition that relies on humor to survive and is difficult to transcribe while retaining nuance and rhythm. As a Jew writing in an acquired language, I may split infinitives, separate subjects from verbs, or use gerunds in the wrong place. Or I may write in a syntax that is grammatically incorrect yet culturally located within the immigrant Jewish experience. English — the language of forced assimilation — is not the essential language of my people.

When I write, existential fatigue of a particularly Jewish nature threatens to consume me, because the life-saga of my people exceeds the limits of my imagination. What could I possibly say that would illuminate the situation? Less than fifty years ago Eastern European Jews were rounded up, our arms were tattooed with four digit numbers; we were gassed in showers and baked in ovens. Gold was extracted from our teeth and surgical experiments were routinely performed on our bodies, while boat loads of starving Jews were turned away from these united shores. Less than fifty years later, the government of Israel ghettoizes an entire people, closes schools and universities; Jewish soldiers just follow orders, bulldoze Palestinian houses and fight stones with guns. Today in my search for story, traditional literary conventions have become useless; creative irony eludes me, and my plots lack resolution. I have lost all fictive pretense. Out of cultural necessity, those artificial boundaries artfully constructed between writer and reader have all but disappeared from my work. When I write, I seek to explode the boundary of the page. Formlessness is the real challenge.

While those who once were occupied become the occupiers, I wait for the mutuality of recognition between the sons of Abraham. Brother to brother, I wait for Isaac to see Ishmael and be seen. This is my story; of what else can I write? I wait for the sounds of laughter; of Sarah and Hagar returned to each other, side by side in the desert wind.

And the living story is filled with symbolic impossibility too deep to decipher, as a nation of survivors carry gas masks made in Germany while waiting in the terror of sealed rooms for a dreaded chemical attack. When the first SCUD missiles land in Tel Aviv — a working-class neighborhood inhabited by Jews of color, of Iraqi descent — Palestinians living under curfew and originally denied gas masks run out into their occupied streets shouting "Kill the Jews!" In this moment, the hope I have for the liberation of lesbian and gay people of all classes and colors clashes with the hopelessness I feel for the isolation of my people. I am a Jewish lesbian writer in mourning for a people who have lost the integrity of their vision. For the first time in my life, I am without metaphor. But because I am a Jewish lesbian writer I must bear witness. In their terror my people have lost their minds, but what about their memories?

I want you to know me, not only as a lesbian but as a Jew. To understand those places of intersection and disconnection where lesbian and Jewish identity impact on my writing. Familiarize yourself with the ways of my people. Ask me about the cost of white-skinned privilege and Jewish invisibility. I seek recognition and dialogue from assimilated, religious, secular, culturally identified & politically active gay, lesbian and bisexual Jews; straight, heterosexual mainstream Jews, white gentiles, the working-class, women and men of color; Israelis and Palestinians. As a lesbian, I do not want my work marginalized by the Jewish community or trivialized by gays and lesbians because I am a Jew. The voices of lesbian and gay Jews belong within the parameters of a multicultural gay literature. The consequences of being seen as white and not also as a Jew is that

I am never actually seen at all by the viewer. This infuses my writing with the surreal as I stretch the limits of reality on the page.

Finally, we return to dinner with the Felmans; to the family table split in half. We return to the surreal image of those who eat the forbidden and fall off the left side of the table. I watch my sisters fall silently through the floor of the restaurant to wander in orbit forever. You will understand then, that it became impossible for me to give up eating chicken when I became a Jewish lesbian vegetarian. Eating chicken is the ritualization of my identity as a Jew; when I ate only green things from the earth, I began to forget the smells of my mother's kitchen, and my grandmother's kitchen. I began to forget that being a Jew was about remembering. Everything.

Hot Chicken Wings

O

Absence

I remember. There was no money for silk. My dress was yellow, a pressed smooth cotton with a tight waist. My fiancé gave me a silk sash, purple, to collect my auburn hair. I wore the purple around my waist, leaving my hair long and open. I smelled the sweet pink ham sliced thin, surrounded by chilled yellow asparagus with Mother's hollandaise. Seated at the dining room table for over an hour, the entire family waited for the aunts.

We ate without them. What choice did we have? The nuns from my school came to celebrate my engagement. It was a high honor for our family to be visited, in person, by the Church. The nuns did not socialize often. I thought perhaps they would resent my plans for marriage. But they presented me with a rosary strung in tiny red rubies. They had wanted to meet the aunts; there was in the Church great curiosity about my family. We lived in Hamburg.

Mother was herself, acting as though nothing at all had happened; that it was quite usual for her sisters not to show up when invited. But I knew differently. I would not forget their absence, nor the absence of a gift. They were the wealthiest members of the family, marrying far above Mother, never offering a thing to us, their own sister's children.

It was so obvious, them not being there, and not sending a note or package instead. No mention was ever made of their empty places. We simply ate for them, enjoying an extra slice of ham, more hollandaise, filling ourselves. Actually it was too much food for Wilhelm, but we kept eating until their portions were gone. Every bit. It had all cost so much. In the twenties, portions were small; food was over-priced. After the meal the nuns led us in prayer, blessing me before Mother and Father. I can still feel their warm hands on my head after all these years; their blessing keeping me safe until now.

I was only fifteen. I was terrified although I was in love. Wilhelm was thirty-one. He planned to take me away from my parents. We were all together one last time before he left for the States to find work, housing. He wanted to settle himself before sending for me, his bride-to-be. He left the very next day.

After the engagement party I did not see him for three years. We wrote every day, full, detailed accounts of our separate lives. Small, unimportant details — like opening the window to check the temperature outside — became significant. Can you imagine, a young girl, separated, so far away from her not-yet lover?

It was then that Mother took in the boarders. She had no choice. We doubled up; my brother and I shared a room, the smallest one in the flat, in the back without a window, barely large enough for one. It was horrible. I was an engaged woman!

We were part of the bourgeoisie, but at the time of my engagement Father was already ill. We had to conserve. Mother gave over the upstairs to the boarders while the family crowded together below. We lost our sitting room, a small upstairs parlor with the upright piano that Mother played the church hymns on. Even the pink geraniums, sitting in the window ledge off the parlor, came under the province of the boarders. I was no longer permitted upstairs to water my small garden. Our meals lost their delicacy overnight. We went from grilled veal to ground beef. Anything from the aunts would have helped.

Mother married for love but her sisters married for money. I was never told this outright, but I was a perceptive child, seeing things between the adults that were never talked about. First of all it was in the jewelry. Mother had only a gold wrist watch, given to her by Father at the time of their engagement. Inside, next to midnight, sat a single diamond. Mother said she could never tell time without remembering her husband's face. The aunts had gold stick pins, French watches, silver rings, hand-made ceramic bracelets. Around their necks, sliding up and down their arms, they wore a small jewelry store.

I was marrying for love. There was no doubt in my mind nor anyone else's for that matter. From our first meeting — standing in the heat as I turned around in the queue for stamps at the post office — Wilhelm returned my gaze with a single nod. In that nod I knew I had been acknowledged, separated and selected from all the other pretty girls waiting to buy stamps. After that we could not look at each other, only he was so handsome I could not bear to turn my eyes away. The air between us was stifling; it had nothing to do with the temperature. Even at fifteen I had knowledge of the heat of my own body. Before leaving, Wilhelm turned around, his right arm extended in a frenzied gesture. I thought perhaps he had left his stamps behind and was motion-ing to the clerk. But he grabbed my hand. In an instant our fingers locked together as though in prayer, sealing the life we were to have, the fierce passion that would live between us. It was obvious even to strangers! We became engaged without delay. We were together only six months before he left.

My love for Wilhelm separated me from the aunts. Until today, I could slice the brie without remembering them. I used to slice cheese for Wilhelm, add brown figs from Morocco, placing the sweet brown fruit on the side of his plate, next to the green mint leaves he brought me each day from the garden. Never once did I think about the aunts. Before the maid arrives, I want to put my memory at rest, to hold only the picture of my dear Wilhelm beside me. I want nothing in the way of the end of my days. My appetite has dried up; it is not just the brie that is without flavor. I cannot die this way.

We were Jews, all of us. Only we did not practice. Growing up I knew nothing of the Jewish faith. I was the the product of an altered faith, the first generation to revere the new scripture. As part of their marriage vows, my parents embraced the Church. They were welcomed so long as they promised to teach their children complete adoration of the Holy Spirit. I know little of my parents' separation from their birthright; only that they craved a home in *Deutschland*. They wanted nothing to do with a suffering past. They felt the customs old-fashioned — the slicing of the son's member barbaric. The Hebrews were an ancient people; we were committed to modernity. I was sent to a Catholic day school. I tried hard to excel in everything; the pressure to prove my devotion was unending.

Mother never spoke to me about her background. I knew only a few details from Grandmother. Wilhelm was a non-believer; he could never have been a Jew. But the aunts observed; they married religious men, lived among their own and believed whatever the rabbis told them. They had no children, either of them. So it was difficult for me to understand why they did not attach themselves to me or my brother. We were the only children in the family.

By the time I was engaged, Mother was working — taking in other people's dirty laundry and taking in boarders. Father was ill. There was no surplus to be had; it all went for my tuition, which was very costly. The nuns charged Mother extra because she was not born directly into the church.

Without Wilhelm, Hamburg was empty. Mother worked all the time. After school I ran messages for the State Welfare Agency and wrote to my dear fiancé. On my way to the Post

Office I would see the aunts across the street, returning from their ritual baths, their heads held slightly at an angle, looking through me. Not even a nod in my direction. They always covered their heads in the latest fashion; they wore identical hats. I remember black fish net hanging delicately beneath a small black box with a big red stone on the left side. At that time I knew nothing of where they had been. Only later I heard the secretaries at the agency laughing about the *Juden* bath houses. I laughed with them.

Sometimes I saw them carrying freshly slaughtered chickens under their arms. They always carried their own chickens, Mother said, because they did not trust their cooks to walk the extra mile to the kosher butcher. Later I laughed under my breath at those two women, all dressed up in fine, black leather gloves, and white silk blouses with lace sleeves, carrying bleeding chickens down *der Hauptstrasse*. They always held their heads so high. I wondered when I was young what they were looking at, all the way up there.

In our letters Wilhelm and I did not discuss them; he did not understand these things. He had no family, no expectations. Once we became engaged I felt that I belonged to someone, separate from childhood — apart from my brother, whom Mother adored, and my father, who made difficult choices for the family. I was not supposed to know, but I did. Later I found out from mutual acquaintances that the aunts knew too. Just the three of us. They knew the innkeeper from Cologne, where Father stayed the first of each month. I knew his daughter.

I loved Father very much although I did not understand him. He travelled weekly, seeking investors for the bank, leaving us alone. It was embarrassing for Mother never to have her husband around whom she was completely devoted to. She made excuses for him; he worked so hard; we must not judge him. She had to know why he travelled so much, but she acted as though he was devoted exclusively to her. Mother did not see what she did not want to see.

She felt only that the bank was unfair to Father; raising his monthly quota, checking his credentials. Father was under extreme pressure to find investors. The Jews shunned him, even though they had enough to invest to secure Father a vice-presidency in his branch. Even the husbands of the aunts refused. So he travelled to find the unaffiliated. In his travels he took advantage of whatever came his way.

Before Wilhelm died, after forty-five years of marriage, I found in the left pocket of his tweed Scottish blazer one of my very first love letters, wrapped delicately in freezer paper, wrinkled and bent where his fingers must have reached for the letter over and over again. I cried in relief that he did not share Father's thirst for opportunity.

After Wilhelm left for the States, I had no one. On Fridays I went to Grandmother's. Often the aunts were there; Mother never went. Together, the three women lit candles, covered their eyes with their hands and then made small circles over the table. Daily the nuns told us how superstitious the Jews were, but I loved the way the light spread across the table, leaving their fingertips, following their hands. They sang then; I never understood a word. My Mother's sisters with their heads at such a high angle sang haunting melodies that filled the room with sorrow. Their voices made me shiver. I had to refrain from kneeling and bowing my head, kissing my rosary that I carried with me everywhere. It was the light of the candles, with the dance of their hands moving in graceful circles while their voices prayed in song, that filled me with an unknown ache.

One Friday they tried to ask me about Father, about the illness consuming him. How had he gotten so sick? They pried into family business. I knew what they alluded to, but I only shook my head, saying instead how exhausted Mother was from the boarders; how she could use some help. I wanted them to share their wealth, help Mother, care for their own sister's children. But they didn't. I had so few dresses, no hats, not a single pair of fine leather gloves, even though I was engaged to be married.

Why I went to Grandmother's was not so difficult to understand. A dullness settled inside our flat when Wilhelm left; the rooms filled with Father's illness, Mother's grief and the strange smells of boarders. Friday evenings at home were crowded; everyone was there, squeezed into a single room, listening through thin walls to the lives of strangers. At Grandmother's the smells were entirely different: clear, steaming broth with floating carrots and green parsley; roasting chicken in brown onions, the skin crisp, each bite. The braided egg bread, hot from the oven, wooed me in spite of the aunts who came with their husbands. We did not speak of the engagement party, their absence, the absence of a gift. I came to be with Grandmother. I knew that once in the States, I would not see her again.

On Sundays I went with Mother to the grey stone church. It was the only time she left the house for more than an errand. We covered our heads with small circles of handmade lace, ivory doilies. At the exact same moment we knelt together. Surrounded by sweet incense and the deep throbbing sounds of the old pipe organ, we received the Holy Sacrament. At church our voices blended with the others; Mother knew the songs by heart. So did I; the nuns made sure of that. My faith was absolute. The grey stone church was not in our neighborhood. We were gone most of the day, travelling two hours each way, praying for hours, breathing sweet incense. I held in my hands my rosary, strung in tiny red rubies.

After almost three years I prepared to leave. I packed, not knowing what to take or what to leave behind. Grandmother wanted to give me her religious candlesticks, the ones from Friday night, but I refused. The only candles I lit were in the church, below the portrait of the Holy Mother. Mother offered me her shawl; there was no money left. I had no trousseau. The aunts gave me nothing, not even a gold coin for luck to sew into the lining of my coat pocket. Mother cried; Father no longer remembered who exactly I was. Everyone but Father came to see me off. I was not angry at him anymore; he simply could not return Mother's love. So she gave my brother the devotion her husband refused. I longed for Wilhelm; someone to be devoted to me, only me.

I was the first to see the aunts, standing rigid on the platform, waiting as though for hours, both wearing enormous hats with feathers pointing up, straight up. One of them carried a small parcel wrapped in brown paper. They had actually come to the station to see me off. I was not prepared to see them. I felt it was genuine bad luck. I resented their presumed intimacy, as though they would miss me. Their dresses were spectacular, pure silk, dark purples trimmed in black lace. I thought of my small trunk, filled with Wilhelm's letters and little else. Mother hugged me. I turned to board the train and heard them say louder than was needed, "Remember your parents! *Dein Vater und deine Mutter!*"

I was beside myself with anger. How dare they spoil my departure with a warning not to forget my parents! I was going to meet my fiancé, to be married in New York City. I had waited for three years! It was as though they had set on my life a curse that I would search the rest of my days to undo. Just as I boarded the train, they stepped forward, the feathers moving first; one of them reached out, thrusting into my hand a small parcel wrapped in brown paper. She did not look at me; she only pushed hard the parcel into my hand, then backed away.

I did not look back but their words stayed thick in my ears; I hear them now this very minute. I see their hats, the huge feathers waving up and down. This morning when I tried to slice thin the brie, all I could see were huge feathers waving up and down, admonishing, berating, accusing. I had to hold my shaking hand still so as not to slice thin my index finger.

But on the train, once my anger had retreated, I chose to open the brown paper. Sitting on a single, white cloth doily was a smooth, round, two-inch wedge of the most expensive brie available in all of Hamburg. I recognized the brand, Gold Seal, and the red ribbon tied around the cheese. When I pushed my fingers into the soft, perfectly ripe cheese I imagined eating the entire wedge myself, bite by bite. I would offer none of it to the other passengers. It was my own Gold Seal brie. I was going to enjoy the entire wedge alone. As I brought my fingers full of the thick cheese up to my mouth, my ears began to pound. I opened my mouth, wiped the rich spread on my tongue, and swallowed slowly. But my throat caught tight; I could not swallow. I heard instead the words "Remember your parents!" Gagging, I spit out the entire mouthful right into the empty seat next to me.

When Wilhelm met me at the boat nearly three weeks later, I decided to push their words to the back of my mind, far away from the life that lay before me. I said nothing that would burden our life together. I had waited too long for this moment. He was so handsome; more than I remembered. He held in his hands a bouquet of yellow roses. Yellow was my favorite color. He wore a navy blue beret angled just above his right eyebrow; the same hat at the exact same position that he wore when we first met in the queue for stamps at the post office. His eyes searched my face for signs of change; I was by then eighteen. It was with our fingers that we actually met, reassuring each other with a firm grip that our love and its heat were not lost.

We went at once to a waiting taxi. After one stop at City Hall, we arrived at the Waldorf Astoria for champagne, *Dom Perignon*, and later, dinner in our room. I remember the long black bottle, completely opaque, that held the sparkling liquid. It was the first time in my entire life that I tasted champagne. There were two tall, exquisitely thin glasses rimmed in gold, chilling in a separate silver bucket. We held our glasses high for a single, short moment but we did not click the glass together. That was something neither of us would have done; it lacked sophistication. We held our glasses side by side, still in the silent room. Then we drank the chilled, bubbling intoxicant, swallowing forever the years of our separation.

In our room, alone for the first time since I was fifteen, we sat side-by-side on a pale peach velvet couch. I sliced away from the whole, a wedge of thick camembert, placing a small bunch of purple grapes next to the cheese. I handed the plate to Wilhelm, as though I had done this a thousand times. We were having our first meal together as husband and wife. I spoke with the confidence of a married woman. I told Wilhelm that I must have a maid. I refused to both houseclean and wash clothing. I chose instead to protect my hands.

Two days later we left New York City for Westchester County, White Plains. I was able to engage a German woman to clean the house and do the wash. Wilhelm had set up gardens with greenhouses; he was growing flowers and fruit trees — apples and pears — for a living. He worked long hours, pruning dark green rose bushes. I was alone a great deal. I thought of Mother caring for Father. But I was a married woman now, expecting my first child. Mother wrote once a month, in much detail she told me of her life. She no longer received the Holy Sacrament; she could not go alone to the grey stone church. Her sisters travelled, she said, bringing back exotic weavings, velvet pillows; rich, cream-centered bittersweet chocolates. Once they sent Mother a box of miniatures — cream caramels topped with a single whole almond. Each caramel was individually wrapped in soft, pale blue tissue, tied with a braided silver string. I never heard from them; they did not write or send even a postcard with a foreign stamp.

I raised two daughters; cared for Wilhelm. After fifteen years in the States I had grown from a young girl into the shock of mature womanhood. Today when I look in the glass, I hardly recognize myself — a grown married woman, widowed, with memories. I remember the days in Hamburg, before the boarders, watering pink geraniums from the upstairs parlor window, looking out into the street and feeling safe. Once in the States I mourned my family from a distance; my parents, Grandmother, all died within five years of my departure. By that time, my brother had moved to New York City, but I did not see him. I had not seen my brother since I was a young girl in Hamburg. We were never close; he was my mother's son. Only the aunts were left, of whom I heard nothing.

I was wedded to Wilhelm. That was my choice; my obligations were to him, our family — my two daughters. That was how it was supposed to be; Mother was devoted to Father all her life. So when we heard news of the shift in government, I did not think much about it. We heard so little actual information, few real facts. We simply did not know what was happening. What we did hear — confiscation of property by the State — was hard to believe. The bourgeois had always embraced individual ownership and enjoyed total government backing.

My daughters went to Catholic school. The bus picked them up within a block of our house; they wore brown uniforms with red vests and matching berets. They marched in the school band. The gardens were finally prospering; Wilhelm developed a strain of roses, tangerine in color — mixing yellow, light pink, deep red. In flowers, he made a name for himself. We prepared for our first trip abroad; we planned to stop at Giverny, to see Monet's gardens — the colors. Wilhelm was committed to strengthening the color of his roses. He wanted to see firsthand, from someone who had understood, the supreme relationship of color to nature.

I had many dresses, some purple, all silk. Thursdays we dined out. Saturdays we entertained. I employed a cook, a German girl from the provinces. On Sundays we ate sliced ham, chilled yellow asparagus with Mother's hollandaise. I insisted the cook learn by heart Mother's recipes. Whenever I was homesick for *Deutschland* and the grey stone I reached silently into the right hand pocket of my robe to roll between my fingers the string of tiny red rubies that was still my rosary. I was finally adjusting to married life, after fifteen years, when the letter arrived.

They said they wanted to visit us — me. They wanted to get to know the children now that they were grown. They must visit soon. They longed for family and wanted me to write that there was a place for them here, with us, with the children. Write quickly, they said. There is little time for preparation.

What could I do?

I kept the letter in my pocket for three days. I read it only when our daughters were in school and Wilhelm was watering the roses. I read it alone, weighing my choices; my marriage, my mother's sisters, their husbands. My husband, the strain of tangerine roses — all the wedges of thick cheese sliced thin.

Wilhelm had worked so hard for everything; the roses were just budding. Finally, we had money enough for travel. We wanted to enjoy ourselves. Wilhelm was already becoming an old man; he was close to fifty. But I was still young and needed to enjoy myself. I had waited so long to live my life. I had had my children. They were taught by the nuns. So that is what they knew.

Wilhelm asked if I was sick; he noticed a change in my face, my coloring. He was always sensitive to nuances, shades of light and dark. I assured him I was fine, only that I needed a rest and was looking forward to the two of us travelling alone, without the children. I said nothing. I destroyed the letter; I did not reply. What could I do, have them come to live with us? My brother had no money; we did not speak to each other. They were depending on me, after all these years. Was it fair?

Besides, I did not know exactly their situation. We did not live among Jews; we lived among our own. We were concerned about many other things — our children and their education, saving money for retirement. There was no room; we were a young family. I did not want boarders. Our world was only as big as the neighborhood; we did not hear news of outside, like it is now all the time on the radio and TV. We absolutely did not hear anything catastrophic. I am speaking about then. Then we heard little to alarm us.

Of course we postponed our travel plans when word leaked out that the borders were not safe. Wilhelm refused to take any chances. When the war was actually over, in the spring, just as the new strain of tangerine roses began to bloom in full, we heard in great detail about the trains, the camps, the deportations. I saw pictures, black and white photographs. I found out their property had been seized. That they had been transported to the countryside. How could I have known?

They were old by then, turning sick with arthritis. They would have died soon anyway. They lived a very good life, plenty to eat, fine clothing, lots of travel. And at the theater... always first-class seats, private booths, with champagne sparkling at intermission. There was nothing they did not have. They lived long enough, enjoying more than their share. It was simply my turn. It makes perfect sense; their time had come. The end had very little to do with me.

I want to finish before the maid arrives. I am almost out of time. When I rise from this chair, I want to know that my appetite will return; that when I close my eyes I will see my dear Wilhelm, our life together and a fresh bouquet of yellow roses. When I reach to slice the brie, my hand freezes in place. I am afraid I will cut myself. This must stop. With my hand stopped rigid in front of the brie, I see myself at age thirty-three, receiving the letter; and I see myself now close to their age, past seventy. They are waiting for a reply. I am waiting now.

I cannot save them; neither could I stand forever at the window watering pink geraniums, looking down at the street below, watching the people go by. I believe the end had very little to do with me. First there was the engagement party, then the absence of a gift; that was the beginning of the end. Theirs and mine. Only we did not know it, none of us. I have remembered everything. The maid will be here any minute; she is stopping at the florist. I have ordered yellow roses for today. An entire bouquet.

O

Crisis

Last week Sheila Rebecca Greenblatt unplugged her phone. She had been in severe psychic pain for weeks. She did not want to see anyone, not even her girlfriend, Hilda Schwartz. Sheila did not know where the pain had come from. She wondered if the pain was Jewish because she had finally cut herself off from the *goyim*. But then Schwartzie couldn't get through to her either.

Wednesday night after plugging her phone back in, Sheila picked up the receiver and asked for help. She called Alice Blakely, a name she had picked from an alphabetical list of local therapists in the yellow pages. There had been nine women listed as professional therapists, but only Alice Blakely had had an opening that week. Sheila had swallowed hard before telling her new therapist that she was a lesbian. She had coughed and couldn't get the words out when she tried to tell the woman that she was a Jew. An appointment was set for 9:15 Friday morning. Sheila hoped she could wait that long. After she put the receiver down she unplugged the phone again.

Friday morning she drove slowly. How was she going to explain her condition to a total stranger? Sheila wanted to be specific. "I'm in crisis," seemed a good place to start. Turning onto Bullard Pasture Road, she counted the houses. One, two, it was the third blue house on the left. A huge German Shepherd came leaping out from the side of the house, ready to pounce on Sheila as soon as she opened the car door. It was definitely insensitive to have a barking dog leaping out at your clients.

As soon as she turned the motor off, Sheila noticed that the dog stopped moving. The least Alice could have done was warn her. She got out of the car without taking her eyes off the animal and continued to stare at him until she reached the side of the house. Nothing happened. Sheila opened the door and sat down on the couch. She was in a waiting room.

The dog had slowed her down; it was already ten after nine. She needed the extra few minutes to think about what she was going to say. "I've been depressed for a long time," sounded better than "I'm in crisis." After all she didn't have any real proof of her depression except that she had unplugged her phone. She didn't know what was wrong with her, but her relationship with Schwartzie was absolutely not the issue. If there was one thing Sheila Rebecca Greenblatt knew about herself it was that she loved loving Jewish women. Even that didn't sound right.

On the table next to the couch she noticed several diplomas in cheap black frames. They were stacked one on top of the other, like magazines in her dentist's office. Sheila had never seen diplomas displayed that way. She picked up the top one. ALICE BLAKELY IS HEREBY AWARDED A MASTER OF SCIENCES DEGREE IN SOCIAL WORK. Social Work. Alice had said nothing on the phone about what Sheila called social working. Sheila pictured herself talking to someone who went into people's homes looking for poverty and child abuse. She could almost hear the woman's soft knock on the inner-city door, her arms full of Shop & Save groceries. Sheila knew she needed a therapist, not a saint.

She continued reading, THE TOWN OF CONWAY, NEW HAMPSHIRE, HEREBY AWARDS ALICE BLAKELY A CITATION FOR EXCELLENCE IN HER FIELD. SHE IS AN EXEMPLARY CITIZEN. This woman did not seem to be what Sheila had in mind. She needed more than a good samaritan to get her out of crisis. She needed a strict disciplinarian. Somebody compassionate, smart, but not too nice. Sheila hated nice women.

The last degree confused her the most. The document testified that Alice Blakely had completed a course in T.A. So she was no longer a social worker, she was a Transactional Analyst. Sheila noticed that she had only completed the course last year. Sheila did not feel like being a guinea pig. She was afraid of experiments. The mice always ended up dead or with cancer.

The door in the waiting room opened. A pale white woman with graying blond hair walked in. A WASP, Sheila choked. She should have known better. After all, how many Jewish therapists were there in Conway? How many Jews were there in New Hampshire? Sheila Rebecca Greenblatt had not adequately prepared herself for talking to a gentile. On the phone these things never registered. She could never tell how white someone was on the phone.

Sheila watched Alice Blakely hold her pale hand directly in front of Sheila's waist, waiting for Sheila's Jewish hand so they could shake together.

Sheila swallowed. She liked that the woman was clearly middle-aged; she had wanted to talk to an older woman. Sheila shook Alice's hand with vigor. She wanted to let Alice know that she was totally committed to working with her.

"You must be Sheila. I'm Alice Blakely. I hope you weren't waiting long."

"Hello." Sheila was not going to mention that Alice's dog had accosted her. She did not want her new therapist to think she was afraid of animals. Sheila followed Alice into her office.

Alice Blakely's plump little body reminded Sheila of her big sitting-up pillow.

"I can't sit too close to you. I'm just getting over a cold," Alice said, as she pushed her chair what seemed to be yards away from Sheila. Alice didn't want to sit close to her clients, Sheila thought, because she was afraid of catching depression. To Sheila, the distance seemed more WASPy than anything else. When the Jews had a cold they all sat around blowing each other's noses. In fact, Sheila had seen her own parents share the same square white handkerchief. But this was not the first time a WASP had had a cold and refused to sit next to her. Sheila knew how to respond. She pushed her chair as far away from Alice's as possible, trying to show that she was sympathetic to the situation.

Once both women were seated, Sheila looked around the room. It was more like a den or a playroom for kids than a counseling room. A huge playpen filled with stuffed animals was off to the left side of the sitting area. There was a blackboard on an easel near the couch. Colored chalk was in the tray with the erasers. Sheila tried hard to get the feel of the room. But she was unable to get one single sensation. Alice sat up, blowing her nose. In a minute, Sheila knew, her hankie would be neatly returned to that place directly beneath Alice's watchband where women-with-colds tucked their white lace hankies.

Alice sniffed. Sheila looked for a cross around her neck. None. Good. She wouldn't be distracted. There was nothing worse than talking to a woman with a silver cross around her neck. Sheila could never concentrate whenever she saw Christian jewelry. She always felt as though she were being converted.

"I'm depressed. I think I'm in crisis." Sheila looked at Alice who was nodding her head with only her neck. Sheila wondered if this was Alice's listening pose. The Jews listened with their whole bodies. They pushed their chairs in closer the more interesting the story became. They folded and unfolded their hands. Alice Blakely listened more with her head. Her entire body remained motionless. She looked as though she was sleeping with her eyes open.

"I feel self-destructive," Sheila said. She saw Alice blink. "It's nothing to worry about. I'm used to the feeling by now. I can usually recognize it before I do anything drastic." Alice's mouth had opened several times and then closed immediately. Sheila wasn't sure if she was gasping for breath or trying to interrupt with a good therapeutic question.

"That's not what I really want to talk about. I just wanted to give you some background. I've been unhappy for days. I can't seem to shake it." Sheila had started talking with her hands.

"Could we get back to the self-destruction?" Alice was taking notes. Sheila watched Alice underline the word self-destruct. She smiled to herself; it felt good to be taken seriously. She also liked talking about depression. Besides the Jews, it was — unfortunately — the one topic she knew a lot about.

"I've always thought if I was going to kill myself, I'd take rat poison. I remember learning in Hebrew school that the Jews of Warsaw carried cyanide tablets on small silver chains around their necks. When they couldn't defend themselves any longer they went down below the city to the sewers and swallowed the poison in private. They didn't want the army taking credit for their deaths. I want to die the same way."

"You're Jewish?" Alice said the word Jewish very loud. Sheila sensed she didn't say the word often.

"Yes, I am a Jew. I like being a Jew. That has nothing to do with why I'm here." Every time Sheila said Jew her voice got louder and louder. She wished Alice's cold would get worse so Alice would have to push her chair farther away.

"Why is it you want to kill yourself, Sheila?" Good. She was being addressed by name.

"I'm unhappy. I barely go outside. I've been unhappy for months. I need you to help me." Alice was still writing furiously into her notebook.

"I've got to tell you what I'm thinking. I don't want to upset you or anything." Sheila saw Alice put her pencil down. "It's okay that you're not a lesbian. I can handle that a whole lot better than the fact that you're not a Jew. I mean, you are a woman." Sheila was quiet for a few seconds. "Just what is your experience with feminism? You *are* a feminist aren't you?" Sheila was trying to keep her voice flat. She did not want to upset Alice.

"Of course I'm for equal rights and equal pay," Alice whispered. Her left hand was tucking her hankie further under her watchband. "I do have a daughter, you know."

"What does that mean?" Sheila had not come here to discuss politics. She hardly knew how they got onto women.

Sheila just wanted to talk. She could see herself sitting in front of her unplugged phone, watching the receiver, hoping the phone would ring anyway. She had to tell Alice about staring at her unplugged phone; about not letting any more *goyim* in.

"Well, it means that I support the liberation of women, for my daughter's sake." Alice coughed. "Do you always interview your therapist?" She glanced at her notes. "Now what were you saying?"

"JUDAISM." Sheila bit her tongue so she wouldn't say anything else. She thought she was going to cry. Maybe she should apologize to Alice. But Alice was still looking at her notes. Sheila couldn't seem to get her complete attention. "I think I'm pretty upset about all this. What do you think?"

"What's this?"

"I forget that New England doesn't have a whole lot of Jews...there's mostly gentiles. Every time I....

"Mostly what?" Sheila watched Alice write herself a note in the margin of her notebook. Maybe she was reminding herself to look up more about the Jews.

"I'd like to get back to my depression. I don't want this Jewish thing to come between us. I'm used to being around gentiles." Sheila was going to offer to spell gentile for Alice.

"Do you know much about Transactional Analysis?" Alice had bounced off her seat just like a high school cheerleader bouncing off the bleachers and onto the gym floor. Alice was standing next to the blackboard. She held the blue chalk in her hand. Sheila had no idea why they were looking at the blackboard. She had not finished explaining her suffering. "In T.A. we divide the psyche into three parts." Alice was beaming. This was something she knew about. Sheila stared at the three blue circles Alice drew on the board. Inside each circle she put a different letter of the alphabet. The first circle had a "C" then there was a "P" and an "A". Alice's head kept turning from the blackboard to Sheila. She was making eye contact. "We in T.A. see the human being as though he were in constant struggle between the parent, adult and child in himself."

Sheila wanted to know, who was this "we?" And was this divided psyche a Jewish or *goyisha* psyche? Sheila had divided her own psyche quite a bit differently than the T.A. people. She wondered if she should interrupt Alice.

"The parent constantly corrects us. The parent constantly says SHOULD. We are most unhappy when the parent takes over. We feel forced to behave in ways we don't want to."

That sounded like the Jew in her. Sheila was always telling herself that she should celebrate more holidays and eat less bacon and ham.

"The adult on the other hand..."

Alice seemed far away. Perhaps she had forgotten Sheila was there, asking for help.

"The adult makes responsible choices based on his wants, needs and responsibilities within society at large."

Sheila recognized that her adult-self was the lesbian in her. The most adult decision she had ever made was to come out of the closet.

"And the child always cries whenever he doesn't get his way, or whenever he feels totally misunderstood."

Alice wasn't exactly an artist. Her drawing was all stick figures, but obviously she had perfected her technique while in training. Sheila was trying to figure out her child-self. Maybe the unhappy, depressed part of her was really the child, crying out for help. That was what she had wanted to talk about. Alice had returned to her seat. She looked pleased. She had not blown her nose once throughout the entire performance.

"Did that help you?"

"Well, to tell you the truth, I could have gotten the same idea if you had stayed in your seat. But it was helpful. I can see the child in me takes over a lot." Sheila's own neck was stiff watching Alice's head go up and down. She seemed to agree with whatever Sheila had to say. Evidently honesty was highly valued among the T.A. people. Sheila wanted to scream; why didn't Alice Blakely tell her to be quiet and listen? Somebody had to be willing to tell Sheila that she didn't know everything.

"I think your problem is with the child in you." Immediately Sheila sat up and decided not to scream. "In T.A. we try to isolate that part of the psyche which is suffering the most."

"Do you think you could stop saying 'in T.A. we...' I mean, I'm just not sure who is talking to me. I'd like to think you can make your own conclusions about my life." Sheila wondered if she'd gone too far; she felt the child in her was taking over.

"I'm not sure what you mean, but I can see you are in pain."

"I really don't want to tell you how to run this session, but I stop listening as soon as you say those words." Sheila tried to smile at her new therapist, but Alice was staring hard at her client as if she was trying to make her disappear.

"You see, I was right. The child in you is most unhappy. I'm sorry if my method offends you." Sheila wanted to lift Alice Blakely's round little body off its gentile seat and shake it up and down until the woman yelled at Sheila to shut up. Alice just sat there staring hard and cold at her. She was absolutely the most unreachable human being Sheila had ever met in her entire life. Sheila felt herself withdrawing. In fact she wanted to stand up and run out to her car, but she was afraid the German Shepherd would get her. Sheila wanted to be a good client. She put her hands together and then placed them directly into her lap.

"I have been depressed my whole life. Lately it's getting worse. Can you help me?"

"Do your parents know you're a lesbian?"

"What?"

"Your parents, your mother..."

"Oh no, of course not." Sheila had decided long ago never to tell her parents unless they asked first. Jews tended to see all things they didn't understand as tragic. Sheila knew that having a grandmother who survived Auschwitz and having a lesbian in the same family were incompatible if your parents were Jews.

"What I think I am really upset about is my depression." Sheila said it louder. "I'm depressed."

"It seems to me your mother would want to know that you have found someone to share your life with..."

"I do not want to tell my parents. They wouldn't understand. Besides I like coming home for *Rosh Hashanah* and the *Seder*."

"*Seder*?"

"Passover."

"Oh, yes, that's like our Last Supper, isn't it? About the child in you, Sheila, you seem so unhappy. Worse now than when you came in. It just seemed to make sense, that if your mother knew about you and ah..."

"Schwartzie."

"Schwartzie, you would be a lot happier. Do you enjoy yourself much?" Alice had stopped taking notes.

"Actually, I can't remember the last time I was really happy. It seems to me I have always been sad." Sheila wanted to curl up in a little ball. She hated reminding herself how unhappy she was. There had never been anyone who could help her. She wanted to ask Alice if she understood about her parents, but that didn't seem to be the issue anymore.

"Can you remember specifics?"

"There's not a whole lot to tell. I just seem to be unhappy all the time. I don't know why."

"It is clear. You do not enjoy yourself."

"Yes." Sheila already knew that.

"Do you think being a Jew has made you unable to have fun?"

"What does being Jewish have to do with not being able to have fun?"

"In T.A. we like to go back to the beginning...you know ...Genesis. We feel it's important to understand our roots."

"I already understand where I come from. This is absolutely not helping me."

"I'm sorry you feel that way. I think you are resisting. I have seen this kind of reaction before. Your kind always think you're right." Sheila saw that Alice was determined to counsel her.

"I'd like you to get in this playpen." Alice was *shlepping* the thing over to Sheila's chair. "I want you to get inside and play with the animals."

Sheila had never done anything like this before. She decided to go along with Alice. Nothing could make her feel worse than she felt now. Besides, maybe Alice did know what she was doing; maybe Sheila would be happier after she got inside the playpen. She got up from her chair and lifted her right leg up so high she almost fell over the top bar. Jumping off the ground slightly, she was able to put her foot evenly down on the pegboard floor. One more jump and she was inside waiting for her next set of instructions.

"Good girl. How do you feel?" Alice was clearly happy. Everything was back the way the T.A. people said it should be.

Sheila tried to get comfortable. The bottom of the playpen was hard. She could see why children never stayed inside for long. She was uncomfortable herself. But for the sake of becoming a happy person, she would try to cooperate.

"Pick up your favorite animal and talk to it. Tell it everything you always wanted to say as a child, but kept buried inside yourself instead. We in T.A. do this all the time. We call it reconnecting." Alice was almost singing. She had a lovely little *shiksa* voice. Sheila could just see Alice dressed in a purple choir robe, singing about Jesus Christ and smiling one big grin. Sheila wanted to ask her to stop saying the T.A. slogan, but it didn't seem worth the effort. Instead she looked around for her favorite animal. As a child she had played nonstop with a small tan fox. "I really don't have a favorite, Alice. None of these are my kind."

"Can't you just pick one? I like the giraffe myself. Try the giraffe. Go on, pick it up."

"Alright." The giraffe was cute. His head was about six inches from his body. That reminded Sheila of herself. Lots of times she felt like her Jewish body and her Jewish mind were miles apart. Sheila liked the brown spots on the giraffe. "This isn't working." She put down the stuffed giraffe and looked through the bars for Alice's face.

"What do you mean, this isn't working? Of course it is." Alice was taking notes.

"I'm not happy. I don't feel anything."

"You're not supposed to feel or think. You're supposed to talk to that giraffe so I can observe you. Now start *talking*." Alice didn't look up from her notebook; she was too busy writing. Sheila could almost feel the word *resisting* coming out of her pencil as she wrote. Sheila felt ridiculous. What was a twenty-six-year-old Jewish lesbian doing on the floor of her *goyisha* therapist's playpen? Sheila stood up. With her left foot planted firmly on the pegboard floor, she dragged her right leg over the top bar, and prepared herself for a quick jump to freedom.

"What are you doing?" Alice had finally looked up from her notebook. She walked over to Sheila. "Don't you understand, you have to stay in there. It's for your own good." Alice tried to nudge Sheila back inside. She put her hands on Sheila's shoulders. Sheila was sure Alice wasn't very strong. Sheila counted to three. She centered herself. She sucked in all the air she could and then heaved straight up. Alice fell back. For a moment both women were completely still. From the center of the playpen Sheila felt herself taking over the session, but that was not what she wanted at all. She didn't know what to do with herself. Alice walked slowly back towards the playpen; she straightened her hair. Sheila could feel her thinking. If Alice tried to touch her again, Sheila knew she would spring up and lash out at the woman. Sheila had been listening for too long. She was exhausted. All she wanted was to be held, to have her head massaged gently so she could sleep. Alice wasn't going to let her sleep. Sheila saw it in her eyes. Alice's hands were on the top bar. She leaned over, bending her head inside the cage. She put her face as close to Sheila's face as she possibly could without touching her. In a very loud voice she said, "Get out. You are obviously resisting treatment, so get out." Alice took her head out of the playpen and looked at her watch.

Sheila couldn't talk. She didn't know if she was supposed to get out of Alice's house or just get out of her playpen. She couldn't believe she had almost tried to beat up her therapist. She didn't think she could ever tell anyone. Who would believe her? She thought she wanted to laugh, but she never laughed when she was depressed.

"We have to end now. We've already gone over our time limit. I am going to ask you to do one more thing — not for me — for yourself. It's up to you, of course."

"Yes?" Sheila hated favors.

"I want you to be depressed for fifteen minutes every day until your next appointment. I want you to sit in your room, or wherever you get depressed the best. Keep telling yourself how horrible you feel, think about being Jewish, and then see if you can cry a little. Write it all down and we'll talk about it." Sheila nodded as she climbed out of the playpen and walked slowly back to her original seat.

"I hope I have helped you. Your kind of depression is quite severe. Why don't you come again on Monday?"

That was only three days away. It seemed too soon. Sheila wasn't sure that she ever wanted to see this woman again. "Yes, that's great." Why was she agreeing to come back? Why couldn't she say no? "What time?"

"Three o'clock."

Sheila stood up.

"Do you want a hug?" Sheila didn't believe what she just heard. She turned towards the door. Alice stood in front of her with her arms stretched out, ready to embrace Sheila with the whole of her Christian body. Sheila thought maybe this was a trick, and that if she hugged Alice back, her therapist was really going to try and hit her or force her back into the playpen. Sheila stared hard at Alice. She was wrong. The end here, where Alice gets to offer her client a hug, was Alice's favorite part. That's what she must be known for. Huggy Alice Blakeley. No matter how the session went, she probably always hopped up in the end, waiting to take her client to her breast. Sheila shuddered. That was one breast she could live without.

"No, thank you."

"Oh I should have known, you're not the hugging type. I can see it now." Alice looked relieved. She reunited her arms with the rest of her body. She had probably never hugged a Jewish lesbian before and didn't know exactly what to do. They shook hands instead.

On her way to the car, Sheila told herself to plug her phone back in as soon as she got home. First she would call Alice Blakely and cancel their Monday appointment. Then she'd call Schwartzie and tell her the depression was beginning to lift.

O

Dance

The school principal and I were asked to chaperone. He's married, very tall, slightly grey, bulging at the hips, has kids and dozes off during PTA meetings. The dance was the last week in November. I didn't want to go. I didn't have anything to wear; besides, I'm bulky in the winter. That matters even when you are a chaperone. Chaperoning is worse than going to a dance. You have to watch. Everything.

You have to watch Hillary Wilson tear her new homemade dress her great-aunt sewed by hand. You tell Hill it's okay, come to the girls' bathroom, and you'll sew the lace back to lace for her. But no, the princess sits out the entire evening, holding the torn lace shut with her right hand, pushing the tears back into her eyes with her left hand. Eugene Farnbacher finally asks Hope Pearlmutter to dance. I don't want to watch.

The day of my seventh grade school dance was a bad day for education. The boys were worse than the girls. They swore they weren't going to dance a single dance. Then Hillary said she'd tell her mother, and her mother would call the principal. I knew Hill wouldn't get asked to dance after that. I knew that seven hours before the dance started. I knew all about the school dance even before the gym was decorated. Hope Pearlmutter told me she didn't have a new dress. What was I going to wear, she wanted to know. What was I going to wear? I wanted to look nice. I wanted to look as good as Hillary Wilson's mother would make Hill look, even though Hillary could never really look good. Hope would look the best, in last year's dress. There was no way I'd come close to Hope. She had long straight hair; the kind mothers want all their daughters to have. I have short hair. Eugene Farnbacher has longer hair than I do. Yes, so all right, I bought a new dress for my kids.

"Do you know how to dance? *Dance!*" Danny Katz yelled at me as I walked out of school the afternoon of the big evening. Do I know how to dance? Sure I know how to dance, only that's not what Danny meant. My kids leave out half the question. He meant was I a good dancer.

"Can *you* dance? *Dance!*" He wouldn't answer. I had done it again. Why not just a straight answer? Why did I always have to give them a hard time? "DANNY!" But he was gone. Back into the gym to decorate. I liked my kids, but I didn't love them. It seems to be a healthy attitude to have these days. I mean, if you're involved in education. You have to be able to go into your classroom, shut the door and take over; then, at three o'clock when the bell rings, you leave your students, the school. I took the rapid transit home. From my seat, I pictured in the window the principal's arms around my waist, the two of us trying hard to whirl on the dance floor. Why did I want to look nice? It wasn't my Winter Wonderland Dance; but the kids, they kept asking me what I was going to wear. The dress I had seen weeks ago I really wanted to buy. A sparkle dress. The material was pastel green and pale orange with silver threads meshed into the print. The blouse lay flat on top of my breasts. It didn't wrinkle or crinkle when I moved. A calm dress, a smooth dress, a Hope-

Pearlmutter-should-wear-it-five-years-from-now dress. The sleeves were long — tight — with a scooped-out neck. I like my skin sticking out, my neck and hints of my shoulders. They were more than round, smooth. Elegant. I wanted that peach and melon green dress because it took me far away from blackboards and late papers. But I couldn't buy that dress.

I don't like to show up my students. Lots of teachers don't care; they don't think about it. But I know, when our stories become too good, when our past becomes better than their past, they stop listening. If we take our kids too far into our own lives, they quit being our kids. They find somebody else — a volleyball coach, or the music teacher. Some teachers don't know when their kids stop listening; the kids always know. They move fast, our students. I couldn't buy that sparkle dress. I saw me inside that full swinging skirt, but I saw my kids pushing away from me, crowding under the hidden basketball nets, not drinking the punch because I was pouring, because they didn't know who was under all that fine clothing. They couldn't find their teacher. Oh, Eugene would tell me I was beautiful, Hope would wish for a sparkle dress for herself in five years, and Hillary's mother would be upset by the soft, cool colors. Danny Katz would stare. He'd just stare at all the sparkle. I was mad that I didn't buy that sparkle dress. I was mad that I had walked from store to store until I found the blue dress. A plain dress, an all-one-color-blend-with-the-other dress. The blue dress had long fitted sleeves and white half-moons for a collar; in a few weeks, I'd wear it to school with all my other blackboard dresses.

At home in the shower I played music in my head; my mind went chaperoning. You get away with a lot when you chaperone. That's why people say it's easy. The kids leave you alone. So what if you don't dance; it's not your dance. You're just there watching. I stared at myself in the mirror. Instead of reaching for a towel, I dripped water all over the floor. Did Danny dance? It's not bad for the boys who don't dance. They stand around in packs of three telling dirty jokes. Danny's always tripping over

things. Even over nothing. His legs walk that way. They're long
and start up high, close to his waist, pushing into his buttocks.
He wears Red Ball Jets every day of the year. I told Rosalind,
my neighbor, that I watch for those tiny red balls at the bottom
of his heels. She laughed at me; I never mentioned Danny's feet
again. Danny told me that sneakers always have to be in good
condition, that it's time to buy a new pair when the red balls turn
pink. Good sneakers squeak, he says.

I had never seen most of my kids dressed up. I wondered
if Danny wore his Red Ball Jets to parties, to school dances, to
dance in. The principal and I would have to dance at least one
dance together; I'd rather dance with my uncle. My legs moved
me out of my apartment, back onto the rapid transit. Twelve
minutes later I got off to go to my own school dance.

Every year the theme is Winter something: land, Fantasy,
Magic, Memories, Victories, Wishes, Fun. My favorite was the
year there was a tie vote. The theme ended up just Winter. The
tie had been between Wishes and Dreams. Tonight, huge tinfoil,
six- and eight-pointed snowflakes twirled down from the ceil-
ing. On the stage was a snowman holding the American flag in
a gold belt buckle. Big piles of cotton were everywhere — winter
scenes. Hanging from the walls, on almost invisible, very thin
grey wire were old-fashioned sleds, cross-country skis and ice
skates. The mats were covered with striped, elf-shaped hats and
mittens — in red, patriotic blues, spruce greens. The lighting was
soft, turning blue and pink. Occasionally the colors met; purple
hues filled the large room. There was a bright yellow sun and a
full moon in the middle of the gym. Coming in you saw the sun;
leaving, the moon glowed out at you, all in silver sparkles. The
punch table was covered with snowflakes; red table cloths were
trimmed with Elmer's glue and gold sparkles. Silver glitter from
the moon swam in the pink Hawaiian punch.

The band was setting up — big boys from the high school.
Each year, to earn enough money for the professionals, my kids
sold five hundred boxes of milk-chocolate-covered turtles,

roasted sunflower seeds and this year, for the first time, baby American flags. The principal had offered to be the disc jockey, to come in costume so we wouldn't recognize him, but the kids wanted real people playing their music. The girls always liked the male singers because they wore tight pants. Tonight the tight pants were black pants. Silver glitter climbed up the black legs and circled around the waists. The singers wore hot yellow shirts, imitation silk, open at the neck. They had on cowboy boots and matching ten-gallon hats. But they had pimples. All of them, even the lead singer. They walked, pointing their feet out to the corners of the gym, taking long, slow strides. They warmed up with "I'm In Love With A Big Blue Frog." Nobody danced to that; it set the mood. The kids tried not to be nervous. I watched them coming into the gym, looking around, not wanting to be the first ones there. The song loosened us up. We started clapping to the beat.

More kids came in; I stood in the middle of Winter Wonderland greeting my kids at their school dance. Hope Pearlmutter had red eyes. I thought it was because she had to wear last year's dress. Hope was small; her body had an awkward grace. There were hints of small, full breasts and much elegance in a few years. Her skin was dark around the cheeks. No jewelry. Hope didn't believe in clutter, her desk at school was always cleared except for a sharp pencil and a spiral notebook. She had on white cotton knee-socks. That's why the tears. I could hear Rosalind, my next-door neighbor laughing; I was glad she wasn't a teacher. Even last year's dress wasn't as bad as wearing white cotton knee-socks to the school dance. Hillary was sure to notice and have something to say. Everybody wore pantyhose to school dances. Hope and I looked at each other; "I'd trade with you, Hope, but my pantyhose are the wrong size."

She stared at the twirling snowflakes. "Hope, it doesn't matter. I know I'm not one of you guys, Hope, never mind." I wanted her to smile. "Teachers don't know much about school dances, do they?" She walked away. I felt her eyes, sad, confused

by what I'd said to her. She had to understand; I didn't know
what to say. Her last year's dress was a nice dress, a thick
burgundy velvet, soft and uncluttered. But the white knee-socks
made her look fragile. Her arms fit, sitting smoothly at her side,
only her legs — her knees — stuck out, too big for her small frame
and the knee-socks made it worse.

Most of the boys looked stiff, uncomfortable and mad at
their mothers. About seven boys had on practical black suits: the
since-you-have-to-buy-a-new suit, let's get-one-that-you-can-
wear-to-church, Aunt Betty's-and-your-cousin's-wedding kind
of suit. Eugene had on one of those all-purpose black suits, but
his mother must have been asleep when he left. He was wearing
a bright orange bow tie, with huge black dots covering most of
the orange. "Nice tie, Eugene."

"Yeah, you shoulda seen the one I was gonna wear. My
mom bought it special for this suit. A black one. Boring, huh?
This one, I won at the State Fair popping water balloons. I hit
four in a row. I keep my tie hid in my bottom drawer. So you
like it, huh? My kid brother wanted to buy it off me for a quarter.
It's worth at least five bucks, don't you think so?"

"I don't know, Eugene." I'm okay in the classroom; I can
talk about the space program, health education and teach an
entire Chekhov story by heart. Hillary walked towards me with
her mother. Parents weren't invited, they weren't even asked to
come in. But there were always a few who came to see the
decorations. Then I saw them: the two tiny red balls walking
away from the principal. Danny and his Red Ball Jets. His suit
jacket was a hand-me-down. His hands didn't quite make it out
of the ends of his sleeves, but the pants were Danny's. They bent
with his body; they wrinkled in the right places. He had on a
pale blue turtleneck, no tie. Once, Danny told me that he didn't
like anything in the way of his breathing. In the winter he was
the only kid in the class who didn't wrap his neck in a colored
wool scarf. His hair was all over the place, not curly and not
uncombed. Danny's whole body worked that way. His legs and

arms were everywhere, but he wasn't uncoordinated. The other teachers said he's fighting adolescence. I liked Danny. He asked good questions. When there was nothing to ask, he asked. It wasn't because he was a genius that I liked him; he wasn't anything of the kind. I'm sure.

Danny's best friend Michael Schear came into the gym; he was the smart one, a good-looking kid with black eyes, thick black hair. And answers. Answers. Michael knew about Picasso, The Fire Bird Suite and French cooking. Whenever I cooked a soufflé and played Stravinsky for Rosalind I thought about Michael. He could quote Buber's *I and Thou.*

I wondered what it would be like in ten, fifteen years to meet Danny Katz and Michael Schear at the Gold Coin Coffee Shop for lunch. We'd sit in the end booth, against the back wall. Danny'd buy the drinks. I wanted to believe that Michael and I would have a lot to talk about, that we'd start a friendship. Write letters. Long letters about life, Buber's philosophy; about Michael — us. Danny'd leave before dessert; he'd have to leave. He always hated anything in the way of his breathing; the Gold Coin Cafe was stuffy. Michael and I would stay another hour, to make sure of things. Danny and Michael. Michael aggravated me plenty in the classroom; he was a know-it-all, but more interesting than any man I'd ever gone out with. I'd break through to the Michael in him. We'd order more white wine. That afternoon in the cafe, everything would come out. Most of the class had arrived by the time I noticed Danny and Michael. The lead singer was giving the kids at the dance a pep talk.

The music started; Michael and Jamie Randall were the first couple out. Jamie had red hair, a puffball on top of her head. Michael was attracted to the red; he stared at Jamie's hair in class. I couldn't help seeing things like that. My legs felt the music; I wanted to dance. I started walking; I didn't know where I was going. The principal had assigned me to the punch bowl, but I was almost in the middle of the dance floor. I turned around, my back to the stage, I saw REST ROOMS and a long red arrow pointing out of the gym. I went to comb my hair. My body felt old. What was I doing here? I didn't want to watch Hillary get mad or Hope wait all night for Eugene Farbacher to ask her to dance. I looked in the mirror. My face was set in a smile. An education smile for the kids. I tried relaxing my mouth, to soften the hard line I'd put on for the evening. The bathroom was empty. I wouldn't have looked in the mirror if any of my girls had been in there with me. They knew I combed my hair, over and over, just like they did; or maybe they didn't know. I wanted to call Rosalind so we could go out for a beer. But I was supposed to be out on that floor, guarding the punch, chaperoning.

Hope Pearlmutter had warm, smooth skin. High cheek-bones. Why didn't my skin glow a little? I always wondered if my kids thought I was pretty, if they told their moms about their beautiful seventh grade teacher? I pulled my stomach in — thin. Kids hate fat teachers, bulky teachers. I needed more perfume, kids like teachers to smell good, sweet. I laughed; the whole evening was ridiculous. Most of my kids were miserable out in the gym, and I was in here sweating like a teenager. Rosalind wouldn't believe me if I tried to tell her how I hid in the bathroom all evening while my kids danced around and around in the school gym at their Winter Wonderland Dance. I made myself leave the bathroom. All I had to do was pour punch and dance one dance with the principal. My kids had to find a new partner every time the lead singer sang a new song.

I came out of the bathroom and almost bumped into Michael and Jamie. They were ready to dance every dance with each other; it was in their eyes. Seth Charlamb walked over to me. I hoped he wasn't going to ask me to dance. Seth was short, shorter than I was. I didn't want my head to tower over him. He had a stomach, leftover baby fat. His mother had dressed him for the evening. He looked just like his father; he had an undershirt on — I saw the outline through his shirt. And his cheeks were bright red. I started to sweat; what do you say when one of your own kids asks you to dance and you don't want to?

Your first dance of the night. Hillary had the guts to say no. Her mother told her who to dance with and who to ignore. Seth grinned at me. I thought of slipping back into the bathroom to check my hair. It was a slow song too. He'd have to stretch his short little arms all the way around me. The kids would laugh that I couldn't find anybody better to dance with. The principal was better; he was older, taller; he had longer arms. You want a good partner for the slow dances. For a few minutes, it's nice to be close to a good body. Then, bumping into Seth, coming out of the middle of the dance floor was Danny. He bounced off the floor, his new sneakers gave him extra spring. "Dance?" Danny said.

"Why not?" I didn't think. Seth looked at me sad; didn't I know he was going to ask me to dance? I nodded to Seth, a smiling, sorry nod. But I was popular so I laughed Seth away. Besides, Danny had charm — long arms, a little class. He wore his Red Ball Jets to dance in, and he was definitely two, three inches taller than I was.

We started out far apart from each other. Danny took my hand and kept me at a distance. Where did he learn to dance like that? My father and his father took to the floor that way. He made a box. We went over and over the same square box. Danny moved with the music. I moved with Danny. The lights dimmed; purple hues surrounded us. I looked for Danny's eyes. Danny was looking at the American flag. I stared at his face, waiting for him to look at me, waiting for him to tell me he liked dancing with his teacher. Not just anybody knew how to dance with the teacher, but Danny did. His hands found my waist, gradually bringing me into him. Where did he learn how to do that? Both his arms circled my body.

We kept dancing slowly to the lead singer's dull heavy voice. His arms moved across my back. I giggled; Danny looked startled, as if he'd missed the joke. I shook my head; somehow my head found his shoulder. I let myself take slow, deep breaths, close to his neck, his young skin. His pale blue turtleneck was soft against my cheek. His shoulder cradled my head. Danny stopped to tie his sneaker, and my body filled with a slight chill, a cold sweat with his body gone. I was afraid he'd feel my dampness when he took me back. But he brought me carefully back into the dance. He even held me tighter. I knew the song was almost over. I couldn't believe it. Why couldn't we be partners, dancing partners, just for the evening? Like Michael and Jamie.

When you're with kids, these things happen. But we're afraid. We keep it all to ourselves, because nobody understands. I knew I'd carry Danny with me after the evening; I couldn't help myself. Students get inside you. Then they're yours to care for, to watch. Danny. Michael. I had always thought it was Michael who I was attracted to. His questions had teased me all winter. I moved my head to look at Danny, to try to tell him thank you. His legs tightened against mine; he cuddled me.

The music stopped. The lead singer told us to turn immediately to the right side of the gym and dance with whomever was there. Seth patted me on the shoulder, stepped forward and pushed himself into my arms. "Seth, not now. Later." I had to pour punch; that was what I was there for. But I couldn't tell Seth that. I turned him around, another partner. Somebody was always waiting for a new partner.

The punch table was a mess. Pink punch had dripped onto the snowflake cookies; the candied glitter wasn't sticking anymore. I had to put my table in order. That was my job. But the music started. I saw Danny's arms finding Hope's waist, and Hope's head finding Danny's shoulder. He brought her into him. His arms moved over her back in slow, soft curves. Hope's head rounded into Danny's shoulder. They had a rhythm about them. I saw Danny's pale blue turtleneck soft against Hope's smooth skin. They danced in small, square boxes. It didn't matter to Hope that Danny danced in Red Ball Jets. Danny didn't care that Hope danced in white cotton knee-socks. But I did. I had to take the rapid transit home alone when the dance was over. I always took the rapid transit home. At ten-thirty, with the last slow song, parents would be piling up in the parking lot, waiting to hear who danced with whom, which girl really looked pretty this time. Pretty, good. I wanted to look good. I had wanted to wear my sparkle dress and show my kids that I knew how to twirl fast on a dance floor. The rapid transit would be empty at ten-thirty; I could look out the window. I could feel Danny's arms around my waist, around Hope's waist.

O

A Handsome Man

I.

When my grandfather opened the front door of our house my mother always said, "Your grandfather's here," and so I stood up. Then I waited for my grandfather to walk into the house and kiss me. All the time it happened this way. He grabbed my cheeks between the palms of his red hands, pulled my head toward his huge chest, then brought my face up and smacked hard a kiss on top of my lips with his open mouth. I sat down wiping dry my wet lips. My father's father kissed very hard, but he wouldn't believe me when I told him; he only laughed. In fact, Grandpop laughed at everything.

I didn't know why I called him Grandpop, except that name fit his hard kisses. When I was little I used to kiss my grandfather back, right after he smacked hard his kiss on top of my lips. But later, when I was past high school and gone from the house, his kisses were more than wet. They left my lips stale and tasting bad. When I was older, I waited it out, until he released his hold on me. And yet, whenever I looked at him, Grandpop was a handsome, handsome man.

He was a big man with blue eyes that fought his huge body for attention. People saw his small blue eyes first; they were soft, gentle. With those eyes he was always trying to push the people outside away. But it didn't work because the softness in the center let the outside people see in, inside Grandpop. Only he didn't know, he couldn't ever have guessed how often his gentle blue eyes gave him away.

The big part of him was his stomach. Not a fat-layered stomach, but a rounded solid stomach, as if blown up only around the waist. His skin was red, earth red with lots of rough spots. He told me that his entire head of hair had turned white before he was sixteen and he said he was proud of it. Once, while walking downtown, he was asked to model men's sportswear — lumber jackets; red and green plaid flannel shirts with overalls. He laughed hard; he laughed out loud with his whole body. He had already worn his last pair of overalls, and nobody was going to find him climbing back inside a pair of those baggy blue work pants. He liked his clothes to fit: "You have to look sharp to feel sharp, Granddaughter Jessie."

He wore a hat, a jockey's camel wool cap angled gallantly over his right blue eye. He had a booming voice that scared me when I was young and scared my mother when she was a young bride. But after a while it only made me angry.

My grandfather was Russian, and everything about the man was left over, immigrant-like. He saw the world divided between big round bowls of thick red borscht and platefuls of Kentucky Fried Chicken. He ate from both tables, often dipping a chicken leg into his borscht, and then pulling at the leg until the meat was gone and the thick red soup was left dripping from the bone. He kept a whole side of the table for himself, as if he alone must eat for an entire Russian village. My father always said that Grandpop could never sit down at a table without remembering the brown bread he ate as a child; often a single slice of stale bread was food for an entire meal. Whenever he had swallowed the last spoonful of thick borscht Grandpop would turn toward me to make his announcement. "You sure got a lot of food at this table, Granddaughter Jessie. Eat up. Eat up while it lasts." Everyone would laugh except me.

After parking cars for fifty years, on his sixty-fifth birthday, my grandfather bought his first brand-new white Lincoln Continental. After that, every September when the new models came out, he would trade in his old Lincoln. But they all looked the same to me. The outside of my grandfather's Continentals were always bright white, while the interior was door-to-door the smoothest dark red leather I had ever run my hands over.

He was first in his neighborhood to drive a Lincoln Continental, and after the war, even when it was no longer fashionable, he continued to mow his own lawn. Once my father came over to mow the lawn but Grandpop wouldn't hear of it. "As long as I got my own yard, I got to cut my own grass. That's the way it's got to be, Abe. A man's got to take care of his own front yard or he won't have it for long! No sir!" Once, when the rains didn't come for over a week, my grandfather dragged the water hose from one end of the back yard to the other, and then from one end of the front yard to the other. Finally only he was thirsty, the grass was left moist-alive, and his Lincoln Continental sparkled like new in the driveway.

II.

My grandmother died when I was twelve; that's why I was sad all the time. She had left me alone with my grandfather. She wouldn't sit between us anymore. I was afraid when my grandmother died, and I couldn't speak for days. Everyone asked me what was wrong. I had nothing to say. My grandfather didn't stop crying for weeks after the funeral. His blue eyes filled, filled up and over until his loud sobs spilled out into the room. He sounded hysterical with a huge laughter, as if he had no tears at all. The week she died the family sat *shiva* with my grandfather in the living room of his house. He sat in the corner in his rocker; the harder he cried the more he rocked. When I stared at the corner too long, he looked like a young boy punished by an angry *Talmud* teacher for some terrible wrongdoing against the Five Books of Moses. When my grandmother died, Grandpop's booming voice made the strangest sounds I had ever heard. But then my grandmother had always said that if she died first, my grandfather's grief would surely consume him. She told me that he was a hard man to comfort because his grief went back to a time and place none of us knew.

The Rabbi came over late one afternoon, and for the first time that week, the rocker stood completely still. My grandfather quieted himself; he pushed his tears back behind his blue eyes. He kept his grief from the Rabbi and instead stared hard and cold at the religious man. The room was in dusk then. The venetian blinds had been opened to let in the light from the setting sun. All day the sun had been bright, too bright for a sad, mourning man. But as soon as the elderly Jew came to speak with the family the entire room lit up with the end of the day. The burgundy carpet looked dirty then; the furniture seemed worn. It was the way the end of the day came through the venetian blinds that made the room itself appear dead.

My grandfather stood up; he was tall in the corner, watching as the Rabbi reached silently for the rocker, dragged it out from the corner and then sat down. All the chairs were moved into a circle. Even the hard-backed chairs from the dining room had to be brought in. The Rabbi wanted to say the prayers for the end of the day and the prayers for the dead. He called for the family to join him. I sat at the end of the couch that took up half the circle. My mother sat next to me. She motioned my feet off the couch. My sisters sat together, sharing a single, hard-backed dining room chair. My father stood somewhere in the circle. I don't remember where because he was sad like his father, and I kept confusing the two of them. The rest were just faces, the faces that come each time the dead must be buried. The strange faces filled out the old Jew's dead prayer circle.

The prayer for the dead was a like a long, slow dance. I watched as the Rabbi prayed; his legs bent gradually, moving the holy words into his small, bony chest until both arms shook gently by his side. Then the prayer went to his eyes and onto his lips, and all the time my grandfather stared hard and cold at the religious man. A low murmur started; the circle had a voice. *"Yisgadal, viyiskadash, sh'mai rabo...."* The *Kaddish* was the only prayer my grandfather wanted to say. The sounds of mourning took over; the entire circle bent in the legs, and arms shook at sides and lips moved slowly until all eyes lit with the words for the dead. My father motioned in his eyes that my prayers were too loud. Later he told me, "The prayers of a Jew must blend one with the other, to make the prayer whole." My prayers were much too loud to join with the others, he said. "The dead need our prayers; your grandmother waits now to hear our voices as one." The Rabbi looked around and said, "She was a good woman, I can tell." He left then, and my grandfather spat after him. My grandfather had stared hard at the religious Jew, opened his mouth slowly, and spat. My father shut the door quickly so that the Rabbi had only his prayers to take away. As the door closed, my grandfather's anger broke. "God damn Rabbi! How the hell does he know if your Fanny was a good woman? He thinks he can come in here with those prayers of his and make everything okay again! That won't bring your Fanny back, no sir!"

"Zeke," one of the faces said, trying to quiet him.

"Don't 'Zeke' me... ever!" and he dragged his rocker back to the corner. This time he turned it around so he faced the wall instead of the Rabbi's dead prayer circle.

"Dad, do you think we're the only family the Rabbi had to visit today?" my father said.

"I don't want to hear it. That God damn Rabbi makes me sick with all his fancy-schmancy words."

"Zeke, sit down." It was one of the faces again.

"If your Fanny was here, she'd understand. I ain't never seen a Rabbi like you got here." My mother kept her head down the whole time my grandfather was angry. She motioned my head down too, as if that would quiet the angry words. But on its own my head stayed up — staring at my grandfather. I wondered why Fanny had never warned me how angry he would be that she'd left him alone. Alone in a world that made him furious.

The dusk outside changed into evening, and the venetian blinds were closed. The rasping, metal sound of each blind closing soothed the entire room. Why my grandfather was mad at the Rabbi, I didn't understand. But later that evening some of his rage slipped into me. Only I wasn't angry at the poor old Jew and his dead prayers the way I was angry with my grandfather for spitting hard after the religious man as he left the house, for spitting and booming out at the man for no apparent reason. All my father did was close the door.

No one argued with Grandpop; they only tried to quiet him. They let him have his way, all of them. So I raged inside at my grandfather who vented his own fury at a harmless Jew. I went home that night wondering if Fanny knew about my feelings, about my anger, where it came from and why it had to come to a twelve-year-old girl who didn't know much about anything outside her family.

III.

I remember one early November Sunday, not yet winter, when I was almost eleven. I had the whole afternoon to spend with my grandmother because my family had gone to Cincinnati for the day. My mother had given me all week to decide what I wanted to do on Sunday. But I knew Monday night that Sunday lunch with Fanny was better than travelling all day to Cincinnati. Besides on most Sundays I had to share Fanny with my sisters. But this week, if I didn't go travelling with my family, I could have her all to myself. My sisters didn't care that I wanted to stay home. They were teenagers; I was just their kid sister. With Fanny none of that mattered. What was even better, as I walked up to the kitchen door, Grandpop's white Lincoln Continental wasn't parked in the driveway, guarding the screened-in porch. That meant Fanny and I had at least two hours together. And when we sat by ourselves, we were just two very fine ladies drinking ginger ale and pretending to talk politics, people and a little about the weather.

Inside the kitchen door, on the wall, there were hooks to hang coats and sweaters. I didn't hang my sweater on a hook; I rolled it into a ball and put it on the floor because I was too short for a hook. Fanny was in front of the stove, stirring part of our lunch — the farfel part. Farfel with a little melted butter and a little salt, in a mug with a spoon, was always better than fried potatoes or corn-on-the-cob. It was fluffier than rice, and it was from the old country. I never knew exactly where this old country was, but I felt part of it whenever I ate farfel from a mug. "Put a little more salt in it, to better the taste," Fanny told me as she put our mugs on the table.

We always ate first, almost before we said hello. Fanny understood that after my Sunday morning Hebrew class I was always hungry, and that I talked much better after lunch. So as soon as I came in, we ate. Actually, I was the one who ate while Fanny only pretended to eat. She'd take a few bites from her own plate, then put her fork down and watch me eat, waiting for the perfect opportunity to put more food on my plate.

We ate farfel from mugs, stewed chicken with onions in tomato sauce, and a few cooked carrots. Every week Fanny tried to get me to eat more of her cooked carrots. I hated vegetables; she thought that was awful. We drank ginger ale with everything. Fanny said, "Your grandfather likes it and says it's the only real soda around." I hated when Fanny talked about Grandpop during our lunch. It was as if she had to bring him somehow into the conversation, to make sure I wouldn't forget that they went together. But whenever Grandpop was mentioned in the middle of our Sunday lunch everything changed, discolored by the sound of his name. I couldn't help myself; Grandpop didn't have to be present all the time. I never really forgot about him; that was impossible. Then the ginger stung my throat. The ale was bitter, but Fanny drank hers down and I wanted to be like Fanny. For dessert we filled our glasses with more ginger ale, and from somewhere in the house Fanny found a box of chocolate-covered raisins. I never knew where the candy came from.

After our meal we cleared the table; we wiped it hard together. We watered every plant in the whole house, starting upstairs in the bedrooms and ending downstairs in the bathroom. Then, we sat down to play cards, to talk. We sat up very straight, faced each other as if we'd scheduled this appointment months in advance.

"What do you want to play this week?" Fanny asked.

"Casino, why not?" I said. Fanny always asked me what I wanted to play but we always played casino. That was the only card game she knew.

"You deal, and Fanny when do you think Grandpop will be home?"

"Not for a while," she said. I smiled inside; I sat comfortably down in my chair, relaxed. When I looked up, Fanny was staring strangely at me. For a few seconds she looked like Grandpop; she scared me. Before she ever dealt the first hand, she put the cards down and began talking in a voice that sounded like the old country. Not once until she was done speaking did she move her hard, cold eyes away from my face.

"Your grandfather is a good man, Jessie. Believe me, he loves you more than you'll ever know. More than you could ever love him, and more perhaps than you could ever love anyone. I know you're afraid of him. Afraid so much he makes you mad. But Jessie, he's not from here. He knows another world, very different from your Xenia, Ohio. You have to be careful around your grandfather. You should ask him about his life some time.

What it was like in the village when there wasn't any food and when he had to listen to the screams of his sisters in the night as the army went from door to door. The neighbors adored your grandfather; they hid him whenever there was trouble. He's an angry man because he's hurting like a little boy, but his eyes are good. Your grandfather's blue eyes are gentle. Maybe one day you'll know that gentleness. I want you to understand that I love your grandfather, I love you. But my love for your grandfather goes back a long time. It began in the old country, before you were even born. Jessie, your grandfather is a very special man, and you must learn to get along with him.

"And Jessie, you will hurt your father very much if you run from your grandfather's love. Your sisters, in their own way, will bring sadness into the family, but you with your grudges will kill the heart of your father. Be careful, my love; I am your grandmother."

IV.

Later that month I celebrated my eleventh birthday. Fanny gave me a yellow canary bird. Grandpop gave me a cage. He made the cage himself, out of coat hangers. It had a slide-in tray at the bottom. He painted the tray in soft blue and green stripes, pastel colors that were gentle to the eye. I couldn't ever understand how somebody so angry could make something so soft, so delicate. My yellow canary bird was the only bird I ever knew to have his own, handmade bird cage. It made my grandfather proud like he told me he felt when his hair turned white before he was sixteen. Every few weeks Fanny sent Grandpop over in his white Lincoln Continental with a box of bird seed.

A year later Fanny died, leaving me alone with my grandfather. After the family sat *shiva*, Grandpop started coming for dinner every Friday night, every *Shabes*.

One Friday night he said, "Where's that bird of yours, Granddaughter Jessie?" I didn't want my grandfather asking about my canary. I could never ask him about his Lincoln

Continental with the smooth red inside, about why he bought a new one every year when there was nothing wrong with the old one. "Come on, Granddaughter Jessie, say something, will you? How is that bird of yours?"

"He's okay. Joshua's okay," was all I could say.

"Let me see him." Everyone was nodding, as if all of a sudden the whole *Shabes* table wanted to see my yellow bird Joshua. I left the dining room and went into the kitchen. I didn't want to stand up in front of the whole table, in front of my grandfather. I knew exactly what Grandpop would say. He'd boom out, "Ain't that something! Will you look at that. Granddaughter Jessie sure knows how to take care of that bird of hers. Ain't that something!"

Since Fanny died, lots of Sabbath celebrations had turned sour because my grandfather had to have his own way. Weeks before it was the piano; I had to play the same piece over and over again. Until he was full. All he could say was, "Ain't that pretty. Will you look at that? Granddaughter Jessie sure knows how to make that music box sing. Ain't that something!" I picked up the cage and watched Joshua flutter hard, crazy. Canaries don't fly easily, and so he was scared and didn't know what was happening. "Shh, Josh, it's okay." I always wanted to pet my bird, just to hold him close, but that was the trouble with having a bird for a pet. I couldn't very well hold Josh close like my mother held me. That made me sad because all the time I was trying to figure out how to show Josh how much I loved him.

I pushed my arm out straight into the room. "Here, now you can look at him." I stood in the doorway, unable to come back into the dining room. Joshua and I had our own world; we didn't want to sit at the table with all those people, with my grandfather.

"Jessie, your grandfather can't see from that far away. Bring the bird to the table." My father was talking to me.

"That's right, Granddaughter Jessie. You're too far away."
So I came into the dining room. And again, like the week before,
and the week before that, I did what he wanted, but I lost my
voice. As soon as he started in with his "Ain't that something,"
I lost my voice. Whenever Grandpop would ask me to do
something, I'd do it, but my voice would disappear until his
booming voice dismissed me. I couldn't swallow or I'd start to
cry. "Okay, okay, Granddaughter Jessie, go on and take your
little bird back to the kitchen." I didn't move; I wanted to spit at
my grandfather the way he spat at the Rabbi. I wanted to be angry
in front of the whole *Shabes* table. I wanted to be furious in my
eyes and then from my lips I wanted to spit out all that fury. But
then dinner was over, my grandfather was full, and I had to clear
the table. I had to clear my grandfather's dishes, to put his plate
on the counter with all the other dishes.

As it turned out, my grandfather wasn't completely full. He
opened his mouth, "Ain't that something! Granddaughter Jessie
sure knows how to clear a table. Look at her go, will you. Just
look at her go!" Then he stood up and walked straight out of the
house, until next Friday. When my father closed the door, I
dropped my grandfather's plate and it broke. Nobody said a
word. I remembered then, the piano week. I had broken his plate;
before that it was his soup bowl and water glass. In a couple of
week's time, I had broken an entire place-setting. But no one in
the family said a thing about the broken dishes. Because they
knew I was mad at my grandfather and they didn't want to talk
about it. Only Grandpop didn't know I was angry; he didn't
know anything. I wondered though, about Fanny, if each week
she heard his dishes crashing to the floor.

V.

Before Fanny died, Grandpop used to give me a brand new silver
dollar, shiny and clean, every time I saw him. Sometimes two
and three a week. He loved money when it was new. Untouched,
it was as if his money was worth more. He would reach deep

into his pocket, boom out to Fanny that he had found something and did she want it. But no, she always said to give whatever it was to me. So I started a silver dollar collection. When Fanny died I had forty-eight. I was waiting for fifty; I had big plans for my fifty silver dollars. But when Fanny died Grandpop stopped putting his hand deep into his pocket. He made me think the pocket game never was, and after a while it was as if we'd never played pockets at all. There were other things too. The grandchildren used to get Israeli bonds — one-hundred-dollar bonds for our birthdays and for every Jewish holiday except *Shabes* because that came every week, and Fanny thought that was too much for any grandchildren. We had to hold the bonds almost forever; they weren't worth anything right away. The bonds stopped too when Fanny died; all the games and surprises were over. I couldn't believe that Grandpop forgot about the bonds, maybe the silver dollars, but not the bonds. Without Fanny he didn't want to do anything. Fanny always told us the bonds were for college. She wanted me to go to college for her.

The biggest change of all was when my grandfather decided to get married again. That was worse than any silver dollar disappearing. Her name was Faye. My mother said it was *Aunt Faye* to me.

"Why?" I asked. "That's not her name; I'm going to call her Faye just like everybody else."

"She's over sixty years old, and you will not call her Faye," my mother said.

"But she isn't my aunt; that's dumb. It sounds stupid."

"When you get to be sixty, you can be called whatever you want. But until then, she is your Aunt Faye because she is just a little older than you are."

But I had trouble; my teeth pressed hard together the first time I said more than *hello.* My grandfather married this Faye woman a year-and-a-half after Fanny died. I had to buy a new dress for the wedding. There was a reception in a hotel just like a real wedding. Everybody was happy; everybody but me. I didn't understand. How could a sixty-seven-year-old man be so happy about getting married? Faye looked collapsible; she had spindly legs that I never got used to, and her dress, even on her wedding day, hung too low, over her knees, almost past her calves. The dress was olive, drab green; it rained hard that day, and I remember thinking that Faye's dress made her look as though she was in mourning instead of in celebration. Grandpop bought her the biggest purple orchid he could find. The violet petals covered her entire left breast. All she got Grandpop was a baby carnation: a few white petals lost on a huge chest. The two of them stood in the receiving line, side by side, grinning two big grins, shaking every hand in the room. Grandpop shook some hands twice. He just couldn't believe himself and neither could I. Then they went to Hawaii for a honeymoon, on a ship, and we didn't hear from them for a whole month.

While they were gone, my father sold Grandpop's house, Fanny's red-rose trellis and the screened-in porch. My mother found a modern two-bedroom apartment for Faye and Grandpop. I couldn't picture my giant grandfather living in an apartment. He couldn't mow the lawn when he wanted; he'd have to share the driveway with German cars. The screened-in porch was a block of concrete extending out from the living room with metal bars instead of screens. The place was fancy, modern — with a dishwasher and an air conditioner. There was a man at the door of the building, guarding who went in and out. I didn't like the new apartment, but everybody else thought it was great, perfect for Faye, just the right size. The extra bedroom was for the grandchildren.

The worst part about the Hawaii trip was that Faye brought back the same thing for all the grandchildren. A strand of perfect Hawaiian pearls for us, and the boys got tie clips, one big pearl each. From then on, whatever one got we all got, no matter what the present was. Faye didn't want to slight any of us, and Grandpop thought that was swell.

He liked her grandchildren a lot. Faye's daughter and son-in-law had four boys and no girls. All Grandpop ever said was, "You can't beat those boys, you just got to join them." He was at their house all the time, romping with the boys, and at the same time, Faye was inviting me out to lunch.

I didn't understand how Grandpop could be happy with Faye, with her drab, baggy clothes and her spindly legs. Even her smile was weak, as if she'd smiled once too often. I decided for good after the Hawaii trip, I wouldn't like Faye. But it was hard — I had to work at it and Grandpop didn't care. The first time Faye and I went out to lunch, I didn't say anything. I looked at her, trying to remember why I didn't like her. Alone with her in the restaurant, she was soft, delicate instead of weak. She was strong inside, maybe stronger than me.

"It's too bad you girls don't feel relaxed around me. Your grandfather and I talked about this. He knew it would happen. My grandchildren don't care, but your family is different." I stopped chewing.

"Your grandfather said not to worry; that Abe's always been too good to his girls, and you were just unhappy for no reason at all. He said that he's seen it before, seen it happen just this way with you girls. Something about not getting your way." I didn't know why she was telling me all this.

"And something else. Why do you call me *Aunt* Faye? My legs shake every time I hear that. I am not your aunt, not even your grandmother. Faye will do just fine." I laughed out loud, knocking over my water glass as I tried to cover my mouth with my right hand. I had to think what to say. I wanted to like Faye; it was Grandpop, I didn't know how to like him. It seemed almost that Faye was like my yellow canary bird, and that Grandpop had made a cage for her too, inside this new modern apartment of theirs.

"I don't see how you can live with him. My mother said you never planned to get married again, not until you met my grandfather. You had plenty of chances, she said. You didn't want his money either, I heard. You had your own. So why? Why did you ever marry him and go to Hawaii for a whole month?" I rushed the words out across the table. Not angry, just excited. I couldn't stop. I'd waited almost two years since Fanny died without talking to anyone about Grandpop. I couldn't think. I wanted to get everything out then. I didn't know when I'd have another chance to talk about my grandfather.

Then it happened, almost like that November Sunday when Fanny and I lunched together. Faye looked at me hard, cold, staring. She pushed her frail body from the table; she sat tall in her restaurant chair. She spoke all the while in a strong, sure voice. A voice separated from her sixty years. A voice somehow linked with Fanny's, as if together they spoke to me. "You're an unusual girl, Jessie. Bright and — without meaning to be — you're sometimes cruel. You must be careful never to let your grandfather hear you talk this way. He loves you, maybe not the way you want to be loved, but he loves you. You can't deny him that love. He's earned it, working hard in the old country, in a small village that was under attack all the time. He had to watch the village leaders, the great Rabbis stand by, helpless. I love this man who is your grandfather very much, you must understand. You must not fight him. Be careful, Jessie....And just call me Faye." After that I said I didn't want dessert, but on our way out, I took a whole handful of pastel-colored butter mints. I jammed every last one of them into my mouth, until there wasn't any room left to chew the sweet candy. Each piece had to melt, slowly from my teeth, from my tongue down into my throat. That kept my eyes from tearing while Faye paid the bill.

VI.

The next few years were high school. They were my years, and no one was going to take them away from me. I didn't want my grandfather to embarrass me in front of my friends, or my friends to ask me what was wrong with my grandfather. I didn't want any part of him inside my world. His white hair seemed whiter, while his voice boomed out louder across the table. Whenever he boomed, I gripped the sides of my chair. I pictured him in a village somewhere, booming out at all the plump young peasant girls. Faye whispered while he boomed. When he took her arm, helping her down the stairs and out the door, it was as if he lifted her entire body off the floor. In high school, I longed for Fanny, who would always refuse help as she walked down the stairs.

Fanny had been a big woman, from the old country; she stood tall next to my grandfather. Her bones were big, and her skin spread tight across her wide body. She had few wrinkles on her face when she died. Fanny's peasant body was not all plain; her strong arms and broad shoulders moved in elegant lines, above the stove stirring farfel, watering the plants, pruning the red roses on her trellis. Faye was thin, small. Her beauty seemed newer than Fanny's, more modern. Fanny's cheeks had been red from the weather, from years outdoors, from watering her roses. But Faye's cheeks were red with rouge. She didn't look bad, just different from Fanny. Sophisticated almost. Faye wore jewelry — bangle bracelets up and down her arms, all different colors. I watched my grandfather's blue eyes watch those colored bangle bracelets. She wore matching earrings, three dangling droplets in each ear. Fanny never wore jewelry; she didn't know what to do with it. But the jewelry went with Faye, it made her look fine; and she had her hair styled in the latest fashion, every week. She made my grandfather proud. Fanny's hair was cropped very short, so it didn't get in the way of her work. Faye was Faye and Fanny was Fanny. It was my grandfather, always Grandpop who I couldn't understand.

VII.

Every Friday night Faye and Grandpop came for dinner. Grandpop shared his side of the table with Faye, as long as she didn't take up too much room. He liked to spread out, she knew that; she laughed, taking only the corner part of the side of the table.

All through high school, every *Shabes*, I stared across the table at my grandfather.

One Friday night I had a new idea. That man wasn't my grandfather unless I believed he was my grandfather. Unless I called him "Grandpop" and acted like his Granddaughter Jessie. I decided not to call him Grandpop anymore. After that Friday night, I wasn't going to think of him as my grandfather. I laughed out loud at the table. Then the whole table quieted, as if all along they'd been waiting to hear my joke.

Faye said, "Come on, Jessie, let us in on the funnies."

"That's right Granddaughter Jessie, nobody laughs alone no more, not if he can help it," my grandfather boomed out.

"Either tell your joke or help me clear the table." My mother was already up out of her seat, carrying a load into the kitchen. Everyone was chewing again; for the moment they'd forgotten about hearing my joke.

"I don't have a joke to tell. I was just laughing. Don't any of you ever laugh on the inside? Just laugh, I mean. My friends and I do it all the time. That doesn't mean we always have a joke to tell." I tried to answer the entire table at once. I even tried looking at each face as I spoke. My answer sounded good to me.

"Sure, sure, Granddaughter Jessie." My grandfather rose a little in his chair. His voice rose too. His blue eyes opened wide from inside, and something in the man took off. "All of you are alike. I ain't got used to it yet. Smart alecks, the whole bunch of you young kids. Faye's kids don't have answers like that. Those boys work, they got smart heads on their shoulders. Granddaughter Jessie, all she's got is fancy words, whole bunches of fancy words. Come on Faye, I had enough of this for one night." He reached over to the corner of the table, pulled Faye up out of her chair and dragged her to the door. She whispered as loud as she could, "Zelach, let's not go yet. You're hurting Abe's feelings, and Harriet still has dessert. Zelach, please." But he opened the door and walked out of the house.

"Come on, Faye."

I wasn't moving at all. My hands held each other. I sweated on my forehead, and felt my eyes go sad. He had done it again. That man with the gentle blue eyes had ruined my dinner and ruined something inside me. I was scared. I understood more than ever before just how much I disliked my grandfather. I thought maybe, before high school, I was only a crazy kid with crazy kid ideas. But that night I felt my childhood anger turn to stone, hard and cold.

"Don't mind your grandfather. He got into a fight today with the janitor in his apartment building." My father was trying to calm the rest of the family. "He left his apartment mad at everyone, even Faye. Let's have dessert." I couldn't have dessert. Nobody understood, nobody but Fanny. I looked around. My mother was still clearing the table, waiting for me to help. How could they go on? How could everybody but me pretend to ignore what just happened? My sisters were laughing!

I went to my room then. My head hurt; all I wanted to do was scream. I wanted to be angry like my grandfather; I wanted my family to yell back, scream, holler, boom out all together in one giant voice at the Russian big man. I wanted to hit that round stomach of his, maybe give him a swollen eye. I jumped into my bed, kicked the mattress and beat at my pillow. I crawled under my covers with my clothes still on.

In the middle of the night I woke up, crying hard, wet tears. I had been trying to talk to Fanny. My body was more than tired — exhausted, as if I'd had no sleep for days. I couldn't help myself; I sat up in bed and spoke into the darkness. "Fanny, Fanny, Fanny." The words wouldn't come. I couldn't remember Fanny, her eyes, her voice. I missed my grandmother, I missed her big strong body. And I hated my grandfather's happiness. Why should he be happy? Why should he be different from the rest of us? Why didn't anybody ever yell at him? How could they ignore him? My head exploded; I pushed it hard into my feather pillow, all the while calling softly for Fanny. I didn't want her gone, I didn't want to lose her. I threw my covers to the floor and went to the window, raising the blinds so the moon could come in. Then I sat in the middle of my bed, quieted by the moon. Fanny had always said that the best part of living in a village was that there was no way to hide from the light of the moon. It shone through the windows every night. Often, when the village was raided at night by thieves, the moon had quieted her. I wanted to ask Fanny about the quiet she found in the moon's light, and if my grandfather had ever known that same quiet. She liked the moon because its roundness wasn't really round. She wanted me to like the moon because it wasn't perfect — because it always filled the darkness with light. I thought then of my grandfather, and that perhaps *because* of the moon, Fanny, and even Faye, had been able to marry that man and somehow be happy. I told myself that if I could like the moon, maybe I could like my grandfather. Then I fell asleep.

Saturday morning my family had already forgotten my grandfather's rage. To them, the outburst was an old man's tired body, an exhausted mind acting up. Everybody said so. Everybody but me. Faye called to apologize. I didn't understand why she called; Fanny had never apologized for anything Grandpop did. But Faye was modern, while so much of Fanny was peasant. My mother was pleased. "Faye didn't have to call, Jessie."

"She was thinking of you," I said. "Because she knew you'd made apple strudel for dessert, and that *Shabes* is special. She didn't want to spoil Friday night for the whole family. But Grandpop always does; he's always angry about something."

"That's enough, Jessie. I don't want to hear any more. I'm going to *shul* this morning; your father has an *aliyah*. Do you want to come? We have to leave in about fifteen minutes." Then her eyes softened for a moment. "Please come."

I didn't like Saturday morning services. The old scrolls were taken from the ark and only men could read from the ancient book. I felt left out; women weren't permitted to read from the *Torah*. It didn't bother my mother; she liked to listen to the cantor's rhythmic chanting. She said the slow melodic words soothed her after a hectic week. So I went with her because after Friday night with my grandfather, after sweating in the darkness and waiting for the moon to come in, I was ready to sit for a while. At least in services, my thoughts were my own.

I liked sitting up close to the *bima*. I liked to almost be inside the prayers. In the back of our *shul,* the old women — the real gin rummy players — whispered back and forth to each other all during the service. I was forbidden to ask them to be quiet because they were my elders. My mother said to let them talk. "When you're that old you can do whatever you want." All the time that was her answer. So we sat up front where it was quiet; I waited to feel close to the ancient Hebrew melodies. *My dreams.* Last night wouldn't leave me. Fanny had never seemed so far away, as if finally she had really died; I couldn't find her. Last night I had lost Fanny's voice. Faye had finally taken hold. I couldn't even remember Fanny's eyes, her face. I was afraid, afraid of what my grandfather would do to me now that I had lost my full memory of Fanny.

My mother nudged me. "Your father, he's going to read from the *Torah.* Sit up. Listen." I moved my eyes to the *bima*. My father left his seat, he was on the other side of the *shul* where the men always sat separated from their women. I saw him smile at my mother as he climbed the steps to the *bima.* My father had a smooth, deep voice, as if he didn't even know how to yell. He had never raised his voice at any of his daughters. His anger held always just in his eyes. But the anger turned from darkness to light so that when he was angry, all I ever saw was a shadow crossing his face, as if he too didn't understand. But we never spoke; I didn't know what he thought about anything — about his father, my grandfather. I sat up in my seat, trying to let my father's smooth voice into my body.

My mother sat tall in her seat, as though my father chanted the Hebrew words just for her. A smile moved from her eyes to her lips, across her face and back to her eyes. She often talked to my father that way. Their eyes had ways of saying things no one ever heard. Once I had tried to give my eyes to Fanny. Although at first it made her angry. It happened at one of our Sunday lunches. "What are you doing with your eyes? They look sad, even angry," she said. I smiled, I couldn't believe it actually had worked.

"I'm talking to you."

"Where did you learn how to do that?" Her voice was puzzled.

"From no one, from all of you."

"Who do you mean?"

"From watching my mother, father and, not very often but sometimes, you and Grandpop."

"That's nice, even good. But listen to me and see if you can understand. Men and women, mothers and fathers talk that way. People who've known each other for a very long time often don't have to talk words with each other. But you and me, we're different. It's more important for us to talk, to explain ourselves. Because you are young and I am old, we need to say what we feel. In a sense, we do not have the freedom of a man and a woman who live together out of love. Can you understand?" She looked at me with each word so I would never forget the conversation. I nodded, slowly. What Fanny said made sense. Talking with your eyes was special, and if everybody talked that way, it wasn't distinct any more. But Fanny and I were special; I didn't understand totally. But I nodded.

"You and me," she said, "let's save our eyes for when we need them, for something important." Again I nodded; I was sad, though. There was something Fanny was leaving out; she didn't want me to know everything. I was just past ten when I tried talking to Fanny with my eyes; I never forgot that conversation.

I looked up; the entire congregation was in song. My mother's face was taut, hypnotized by the ancient melody. My father was finishing his last *brokhe;* my mother's lips moved with his. Even the gin rummy players had quieted their whispers.

By the end of the service, I thought I understood what had happened last night inside my head, alone in my bedroom. Fanny had gone away on purpose. I had not just dreamed the whole thing out of loneliness and anger. She was forcing me to talk with my grandfather, without her — just my grandfather and me. When she was alive, Grandpop and I hardly ever spoke directly to each other. He would ask me a question through Fanny, like the silver dollar questions. Or on my birthday, when Fanny gave me a bird so he could make me a cage. But after last night Fanny had left me. She had hinted at this — only Grandpop and me left to face each other without her protecting me. When Fanny and I sat facing each other, playing a round of casino, she had tried to warn me but I wasn't paying close attention. I thought too, that my grandfather was a big man, a peasant, but I wasn't a peasant girl like Fanny. My body was not plump, full and strong with muscle in the arms and in the shoulders. I had a city body, a soft, unworked body. I understood then that my grandfather was old and I was young, so we had to talk before it was too late.

After services my mother and I waited for my father. We walked home together; I walked behind them. Even at fourteen, I liked it that way — as if I was their bodyguard. To the street I was a tag-along child, but to me I was important; I had a job to do. Every once in a while my father turned around. "Just wanted to know if you're still there; didn't fall into the street or anything, did you?"

"Not me." We smiled; we talked with our eyes. "Good *Shabes.*"

"Good *Shabes,*" and they stopped walking so my father could kiss me my *Shabes* kiss.

VIII.

During my last year of high school, I watched my grandfather whenever I could. I watched him eat, drink and boom out commands, and leave when he was full. Every Friday night he was the same. I held his blue eyes for short moments. He was surprised. Sometimes, during a meal, while the family ate my grandfather and I rested. We put our silverware down and found each other's eyes. Just for moments here and there.

One Friday night, at the end of high school, right before college, Grandpop boomed out in the middle of dinner, "Grand-daughter Jessie sure has got the eyes, a pretty set of brown eyes, and boy has she learned what to do with them." The table smiled, not sure what he was talking about, but respectful of his age, they smiled again. I saw that he didn't understand that I wasn't flirting with him. I didn't want to be angry, but he'd misunder-stood everything. He grinned back at me; across his whole face he grinned.

IX.

Once at college, I waited to go home, waited to see my grand-father again. I couldn't grow up until my grandfather and I grew closer. Fanny was still so far away; I wondered if she had ever *really* lived, if all I remembered had ever happened. Now, so many years later, it seemed that Faye had always belonged to the family. Where was Fanny? In a letter I asked my mother if my father still missed his mother. She wrote back right away.

Dear Jessie,

Your father misses his mother very much. He's at the cemetery often, with red geraniums. Usually, as soon as it's warm enough, he goes to the cemetery and cleans around the stone with warm water and soap. He picks up the trash around your grandmother's grave: the cigarette butts and the wild berries from the trees that always make such a mess. Sometimes he takes five red geraniums and a single pink one. He stays long enough to say the Kaddish, Jessie. And he says to tell you that he'll take you with him if you want. When you're home for winter break. Think about it; Fanny would like it.

But Jessie, your grandfather is not well, and that is why I really write to you. We are all so worried about him. Send him a card, won't you? He loves you and needs to hear from you. He hears often from the other grand-children. But Faye says he always asks after you. Why don't you ever write to him? Write him, just a note.

We're fine, the rest of us, but worried about your grandfather. Study hard. See you soon.

Love and lots of kisses,
Mother

The fact that Grandpop might die before I had a chance to get to know him was a sad-funny thing. My mother wanting me to write him, just a card, as if I could create our relationship on paper. My grandfather would never write back, but that wasn't the point. It was as it always had been; my grandfather got his way. He'd been sick before, when Fanny was alive, and even then, pain and all, he refused to go to the doctor. But everybody had to know, had to hear about his sickness. Now Faye had to take care of his sickness. She had to stay home to bathe and feed him, without saying a word. I tried to write a letter; just to make Faye happy, I tried to write. The words wouldn't come. After all these years I had no idea what to say. To scribble a greeting, a *hello* and a *how-are-you, I miss you,* I couldn't do. Just words without a feeling I couldn't ever write. I didn't write my grand-father.

He was at it again; his sickness was no different than me dragging out Joshua in front of the whole Friday night table, just because my grandfather wanted to check out my canary bird, his cage. I had no more dishes to break, I'd outgrown nightmares with moonlight, and worst of all, I wasn't even home. Yet the anger stayed inside me. I wanted to talk to my grandfather, only I didn't know how. Now, his sickness was in the way.

I heard too, that first semester at college, about Grandpop's eyesight. He couldn't see clearly anymore. Faye had made several eye appointments for him and offered to go with him;

even my father offered to go with him. No... the Russian giant cancelled his own appointments. Instead he left for the parking lot hours early so he had the entire street to himself. He drove down the middle of the street at 6:00 o'clock every morning in his white Lincoln Continental. His blue eyes reddened from the strain of peering out of the windshield before sunrise on grey cloudy days. Then he started complaining that the newspaper print was getting smaller and smaller, every day. So Faye had to sit for hours, reading whatever there was in the papers to interest an angry old man. All that made my mother write me another one of her letters.

> *Dear Jessie,*
>
> *If your grandfather's eyesight doesn't improve, we're all going to be in trouble. Your father is scared to death that your grandfather is going to hit some child running across the street. On his way home from work, your grand-father refuses to drive the speed limit; he can't read the signs. And poor Faye says nothing. Why don't you write him? A note, a card? He only eats soup now. Faye's homemade soup. At least once a week I try to make some soup so Faye doesn't have to cook all the time. Send them a card, Jessie, please. And write to us too.*
> *Love and lots of kisses,*
> *Mother*

I never answered my mother's letter. I went home for winter break; I went to see Grandpop, with his big stomach, his blood-shot blue eyes and his white hair. The guard at the door of the apartment building looked at me as if I'd never been to visit before. Faye let me in. "It's Jessie, Zelach," she called into the hallway. "It's good to see you, Jessie. Sit down." She pointed to the kitchen table and chairs.

"How's my grandfather?"

"He's doing much better; he'll be here in a minute. Zelach," she called a little louder down the hallway, "come on into the kitchen so we can talk to Jessie." She looked at me sadly, as if she knew how hard it was for me to be there.

"All right, all right. I'm coming," my grandfather boomed out from the bedroom. The floor seemed to shake then; I looked at Faye, but she didn't notice a thing. It was my grandfather coming towards me with his face stretched to give me a hard kiss. I'd almost forgotten those kisses of his. Then he smacked hard on my lips a very wet kiss. I felt bad again; I had to wipe my lips dry, my cheeks, my whole face. I still didn't want his kiss wet on my skin. The bad taste came back to me. "Sit down, will you? Come on, Granddaughter Jessie, sit down. What do you know?" He was happy, untouched by the world outside his apartment. He didn't look sick at all. He was even now a handsome, handsome man. The anger in his face was calm; but I couldn't believe my grandfather had quieted, had soothed his anger while I had been away at college. Then he started to talk; before I said a word about college, my grandfather took off. Faye sat up. He started in about my hair. I had it curled into little tiny ringlets that I puffed up with a black plastic pick. I had it done as soon as I got to college: nobody at home knew about my curls. That was my surprise.

"What did you do to your hair, Granddaughter Jessie?" He puzzled in his words, as if I was somebody new, so different he couldn't recognize me. He reached out and grabbed some curls, pulled at them, pulled hard to take the curl out of my hair, to pull my hair back the way it had always been. It was short before, cropped short, the way Fanny used to wear her hair. He wanted it back the way he liked it; the way he recognized me.

"She looks cute. Better than before." Faye tried to soothe the situation.

"Cute, hell. I'm glad your Fanny's not alive to see it; she'd be sick in her stomach. Girls, young girls where your Fanny and I came from never did such crazy fool things to their hair. They didn't have the time. Even Granddaughter Jessie's face looks thinner. It ain't got no life. She looks like the *goyim!* And look at the clothes she's got on. Tight across the chest like she's got something for sale. Boy, what college don't do for you girls! You think you're smart, Granddaughter Jessie? Well, that hair don't do nothing for you. You don't look real. You don't look half as good as your Fanny looked, or even as good as Faye looks. You got it all wrong, Granddaughter Jessie."

"Are you through?" I was soft in my voice but I didn't take my eyes off my grandfather. He was so sure he was right. This kind of talking couldn't have been what Fanny meant. She never meant for my grandfather to hurt me this way. All the time Faye had to watch everything. Fanny only *thought* she knew Grandpop. Maybe Fanny never *really* knew Grandpop and his anger. Grandpop didn't yell at Fanny; his anger was for me, for the young. This "old country" they always spoke about had nothing to do with me. There was no way I could be part of their village. Nothing my grandfather could say could make me into a village girl, plump with big strong bones like Fanny.

"Granddaughter Jessie, say something, will you? Faye and I are just sitting here, waiting for your pretty little mouth to open up and tell us about that fancy college of yours." I just stared at both of them; my thoughts were coming too fast. All of a sudden I knew why Grandpop married Faye, to help him live in the present, live closer to his granddaughters. After he lived first in the old world with a big-boned woman, a strong red-cheeked rose-trellised woman, and after they moved to the new world where he drove a white Lincoln Continental instead of a mule-drawn wagon, he was afraid. He was afraid so he made a beautiful bird cage for my yellow canary bird, and he made all the trips to the house with the bird seed. He gave Joshua a home forever and always food. When he married Faye, my grandfather surprised himself more than anybody else. In a way, he gave up the old country for good. Maybe Fanny knew all of this, and maybe Faye knew too. My grandfather and I were of the same world then. It made sense; I'd never understood before. We had no world; both of us were lost somewhere in between. We shared the same anger, only he was old and exhausted from living in two worlds; I was young, without a real beginning. I had no old country to come from, to belong to.

I saw too why I was so afraid of knowing my grandfather. Because in the knowing, my anger dissolved. My grandfather was exhausted from his own anger; I didn't want to be like my grandfather, tired my whole life, mad and furious with the world. So I knew I couldn't tell anyone how he had boomed out, and then torn at my hair. My hair and my clothes were part of my world, a world he would never be able to know. I thought that perhaps Fanny knew; if that was so, she knew even before I did. I wanted to tell my mother, to tell her that I understood it all so much better. I knew why everyone always said my grandfather was a good man. They were nice to him because he was always the stranger to them; someone who needed food and shelter, not a person they really knew.

My grandfather's eyes were on me while the room was silent. I could see that he wondered why I had no words for him, why I didn't match his anger with my own. His sharp-tongued granddaughter was quiet when she should have been angry. My grandfather didn't know what to do. Faye was frightened. She stood up and her legs, her spindly legs knocked back and forth. I saw that her dress still hung low, almost past her calves.

And then even when I understood, I saw that it was still not enough to make me love this man. I didn't want to give away that much love. My grandfather had never really left the old country; he was only visiting here. I loved Fanny though; she had never pretended to live in this country.

X.

I graduated from college three years later, in May, but I didn't receive my diploma until the first of July. During *Shabes* dinner someone mentioned that my diploma had come in the mail earlier that day, and that it was beautiful. Grandpop couldn't believe that I had actually graduated from college; he made me run upstairs for my diploma. He wanted to see it for himself, the facts. That was okay; a lot of people have to see for themselves. But when I opened the navy-blue leather case for my grandfather's inspection, he boomed out, "Ain't that something! Will you look at that. Granddaughter Jessie really did something for herself this time." The whole table laughed as he reached for his billfold.

It was as if he planned to pay back my father every cent he'd spent on my college education. But instead he took out a pile of brand-new dollar bills, ran them between his fingers and handed me one from the middle of the pile. "There Granddaughter Jessie, put that in your pocket." You would've thought he'd given me a million dollars; he created a religious ceremony out of a single dollar bill. In honor of my college graduation, he had made up his own ritual just for me, right at the table. I glanced around the room. Everyone had lowered their eyes as if they too were praying.

"Thanks, Grandpop, thanks for the brand-new dollar bill," I said. But as I reached for the dollar bill with my right hand, my whole body reached forward; my arms went out from my sides as if they planned to hug my grandfather. I realized then that I wanted to embrace my grandfather, that I wanted to hold him very close.

When he had first reached for his billfold, I had begun to feel all this. I wanted a love that had nothing to do with an old country or a new country. I saw too, that for everybody else, none of this mattered; it never had. So they laughed at the Russian big man; they teased the stranger. But I could never do that. As angry as I had always been at my grandfather, I had never laughed at him or even treated him like he was still a child. I reached out for the brand-new dollar bill, but before my arms could reach out to hug him, he grabbed me just like he used to grab Fanny when he walked in the door after work. With his arms around me I couldn't move. Grandpop boomed out, "Sure

Granddaughter Jessie." He was grinning big. "My pleasure! It was all my pleasure!"

O

Jelly Rolls

"Is this where the bus for Durham comes in?"

Edith Jeanne Drinkwater needed an answer to the exact same question, so she turned half a circle around. When she saw that she was facing a fat woman, Edith wanted to immediately complete the circle. But she couldn't do that because the fat woman had got hold of one of her eyes and wasn't letting go until Edith answered her question.

Edith had a thing about eye contact; it was just plain impolite to ignore someone else's eyes when they were aimed at you. So she looked, expecting to see a single big eye in the middle of a huge face. Much to her surprise the woman had two eyes just like she did. And the woman's eyes were the exact same color as her very own.

Unbelievable, Edith said to herself, not because she thought she had the only pair of green hazel eyes in the world; it was just that — Edith was laughing to herself — who would have thought that *fat* women had green eyes?

Before she knew what she was doing, thirty-five-year-old Edith found herself agreeing with the woman that Gate Three was their gate. Edith had never agreed with a fat woman in her entire life. She did not know what to do. She worried that the woman would assume friendship — think that the two of them could share a seat on the bus. Edith knew what she was going to have to do and she didn't like it one bit. She was going to have to force herself to take up an entire row of seats. In order to accomplish that — because the size of her own body was so small — she now planned to spread her packages out over both seats instead of putting them on the rack above her as she usually did.

For the next fifteen minutes — to make her own position perfectly clear — Edith planned to ignore the fat woman. They had absolutely nothing in common; it was sheer coincidence that had the two of them riding the same bus to the same place this very Sunday night. Edith's ears filled up. She knew that fat people always sounded like they were addressing the entire world with a single breath; they did not have small voices. The woman was trying to appear as though she were not addressing anyone in particular. When a young boy finally announced the bus's arrival time, "6:15," Edith leaned over to make sure she had heard right. After all, it was her bus too.

Quickly she stomped her sturdy Thom McAns on the floor of the Greyhound station. She had to keep her body firmly in place. Edith wondered if this woman understood the difference between herself and the rest of the human race. Edith knew the difference; she had always known the difference, ever since she was a little girl, and her mother had pointed all the way down the street at a huge blue bonnet. "That, E.J., is a fat woman; we don't mess with them. So don't let me catch you bringing one of them home for a glass of whole white milk and one of my homemade walnut-pecan butterscotch brownies. Friends like that you don't need — they're contagious." Edith had never forgotten her mother's wisdom. In fact last week she'd decided to point out that same blue bonnet to her daughter, next time they walked down the street together.

Edith felt green hazel eyes hanging onto her feet. She knew better than to think anyone would stare like that at a single pair of Thom McAns, no matter how small the feet were that wore them. Edith was scared. For the first time since she'd entered the bus station, she wasn't precisely clear about what was going on around her. That wasn't like her; she wasn't herself today. She wasn't sure about anything and after a few more minutes of feeling fat green eyes move up and down her entire body, Edith's fear turned into panic. The fat woman was seeing something she shouldn't be seeing. Holding her packages close to her small breasts, Edith begged her feet to move her body forward. It had to be time to leave. Once she got on the bus, she knew she'd feel more like herself.

As she started for the gate, Edith felt an entire army coming after her. There must be some mistake; everybody had begun to follow Edith. This had never happened to her. She was no leader. She knew her place, and that had always been toward the end of every line. She was not one to push her way forward. Thin people never had to push and shove. Thin people were always sandwiched in between the larger people so that nothing would happen to them. That was the way Edith had always seen life work.

She found herself glancing around for the fat woman, who she saw, much to her dismay, was bringing up the end of the army. Because Edith had decided to wait and board last, what Edith had most feared *might* happen, already *had* happened. Everyone going to Durham, New Hampshire, had assumed the two women were travelling together, and that they knew when to board the bus. Edith sincerely hoped the woman would take over the lead; then the confusion would clear up once and for all.

Somewhere in the background their bus was called and the fat woman took over the lead at the same time. Edith had stopped moving. When the announcement was over, the woman's ticket was in the driver's hand. Edith smiled at her feet, feeling almost like her old self again. The fat woman had taken over the responsibility for leading the people home. That was the way all life should be. In case there was any danger, it would happen to the fat woman first. Besides, there was always a draft at the beginning of the line. Edith knew fat people didn't get cold like the rest of them. She had only seen their kind dressed in thin coats with hardly any buttons. That was definitely the only lucky part about being a fat person; you didn't feel the cold. Edith was cold now, and although that meant she might be sick in bed tomorrow, it also meant she wasn't fat.

She had been standing in one place for so long that everyone had passed her up. She was the last passenger to board the bus. Edith gave the driver her ticket without looking him in the face. She was keeping her green-hazel eyes to herself and she was putting one foot directly in front of the other. She wasn't going to look for a seat until she was smack at the front of the aisle. No single individual was going to get this very cold but thin woman to lift her eyes until she was ready. When her feet were in place Edith was amazed. The confusion was still not over.

The problem was that the fat woman had seated herself directly behind the driver, while all the real passengers had seated themselves behind the entire first row. How could they do this to her: leave her up front with that woman? What if her daughter had been travelling with her? How could she have explained to such a young child why they had to sit in the fat section? Edith lifted her eyes slowly; before she took her seat she was going to have her say. She made her eyes go from seat to seat until they'd been up and down the whole aisle; she wanted the people to know that Edith Jeanne Drinkwater knew exactly what had happened; they had deserted her, one of their own. Only the fat woman met her gaze, waiting for Edith to take the row of seats across the aisle from her own row. Edith stared into the eyes of her people. *Thank you, each and every one of you for making my dream come true. All day I was praying for the first seat on this bus. That way, as soon as we turn down Main Street, my daughter will see — even before I get off the bus — that her mother has come home. You are all good people and I thank you.*

Edith had made her eyes carry all the way to the back of the bus. Satisfied that she had excluded the fat woman from her gaze and that she had redeemed herself, she sat down, calmly waiting for the bus to begin its journey. Her own mother would have been proud of her. Edith had seen the heat of the fire coming straight for her, but she'd turned it ice-cold without ever getting burned. For the first time since this whole mess had started, she'd almost forgotten the fat woman existed. With a little more concentration, she was sure she could finish her off for good.

She'd just close her eyes and see if she could imagine the woman's seat giving way. Then the fat woman would be left out in the road. In order to keep moving, the back wheels of the bus would have to roll right over her.

Edith thought she could do it. She'd been in strong control of her imagination ever since she was a child. But when Edith closed her eyes, nothing happened. She blinked fast and closed them again tighter, in case there had been a mistake. This time she concentrated more. But behind her eyes was no fat woman falling through the floor of the bus. There was nothing but the black of the night behind those green hazel eyes.

Edith knew from past experience that some things took more work than others. She would try harder. After all, they were *her* eyes; if she couldn't get them to see what she wanted to see, nobody else could. She closed her eyes again, but had to open them immediately. Clearly there had been some confusion. She would close her eyes one more time to make sure that what she thought she was seeing, she wasn't seeing at all. There was no mistaking what was going on behind Edith's eyes. Food. Lots of food. It was the fat woman up to no good, and Edith wasn't going to stand for it. Just because they both had green-hazel eyes did not mean they had to see the world the same. Never before had she lost her own clear sight and never before had she closed her eyes and seen only food.

The bus was not due in Durham for over an hour. That was long enough to regain her own sight. Edith remembered there had been a single occasion in her youth when her eyesight had been impaired. She had not listened to her mother, who had told her never to look straight into the sun or she might go blind for life. Edith hadn't gone blind for life though, she'd only lost sight for a few seconds. For those few seconds, she had felt separated from the entire human race. That had been the most horrible feeling she had ever hoped to feel. Even as a child she could not stand being separated from her people. Although that seemed to be happening again, only this time right in front of her eyes.

Edith could feel her body resting; she was tired from all the confusion. Her eyes closed. The food came back into view but Edith didn't even try to make it go away. At the same time her small body spread out small across the entire seat. She was careful not to interfere with her packages. It felt good to be going to sleep. She was one of them after all; Edith had seen lots of her people sleeping on buses, spread out in all directions. Everything was going to be fine.

In the middle of her dreams, Edith woke to find herself staring at the fat woman's stomach. The woman had slumped over and spread out in all directions just like Edith had done. The woman had no right to copy Edith's body position. The fat woman was even taking up both seats. Edith could see absolutely no reason why they had to sit in identical positions. She moved her body immediately, careful not to squash her husband's sweet rolls.

Edith tried to bring her legs together before the bus driver looked into his rear view mirror and noticed the unladylike position she'd gotten herself into. But nothing happened. She couldn't get her eyes to remove themselves from the fat woman's stomach. Never before had she lost so much control of her faculties. She was clearly not herself today. She would have to try again to move her legs, because as long as Edith had known her husband he had refused to eat his sweet rolls if they were the least bit flat. Any minute her right thigh was going to flatten those jelly rolls out for good.

Just as she tried lifting her legs, Edith's eyes started talking inside her head. She wondered what exactly was inside the fat woman's stomach. Maybe, if she stared hard enough, she could see in through all that thick flesh. Her eyes imagined piles of white powdered sugar where she supposed the top of the woman's stomach began. She stared harder; Edith laughed to herself. The white powder was turning into a giant jelly roll.

She got hold of herself fast. She did not like the idea of the fat woman and her husband eating the same food even if it was only for breakfast. That meant her husband's stomach could one day look like the fat woman's stomach. Edith knew she could never serve a fat man dinner at her table. She was going to have to act faster than she had ever acted in her entire life. Edith's hand reached to secure from under her thigh the bag which held her husband's jelly rolls.

That was when Edith noticed the fat woman's mouth opening and closing while she slept. It appeared the woman was eating the air. When her mouth closed, anyone could see she was chewing and swallowing. Edith knew eating when she saw it, and the fat woman was eating her sleep. Edith felt her left hand open her husband's jelly roll bag. She knew what she had to do to keep her husband from turning into a fat woman. Her hand sank fast and deep into the white powdered sugar. She crumpled some powder between her fingers while she watched the fat woman eating the very air on the bus. The next time the fat woman's mouth opened, Edith's mouth opened right along with hers. Slowly at first, just to get the feeling of chewing on a moving bus. It felt good; Edith got her jaw moving in the same round motion as the fat woman's jaw.

She hummed to herself, softly so she wouldn't wake the woman. She was beginning to feel weightless, which was not hard for someone of Edith's small size. Her hand caught hold of one of the big jelly rolls. All she had to do to save her man was bring that roll up to her mouth while her lips were parted. If she got it up there while her lips were closed, Edith didn't know what would happen. She might push the roll back into the bag fast and stop all this rescue work immediately. She pictured her kitchen table which was only big enough for three small people. She saw her husband sitting down to his breakfast and getting up too big to ever sit down again. Quickly she stuffed the entire sweet roll into her mouth.

Powdered sugar was everywhere. Edith couldn't see clearly because some of the white stuff was floating right in front of her eyes. She waved her arms, hoping her vision would clear. When she could see again, she saw the fat woman staring straight at her husband's bag of red jelly rolls. Edith said NO! out loud. Faster than she had done before, she stuffed another jelly roll into her mouth. The woman just kept staring as if Edith hadn't said a word. Edith tried to chew faster. Eating on the bus wasn't so bad after all; it helped pass the time.

She knew there were exactly twelve rolls left. She'd bought fourteen — a week's supply. They had all been for her husband, who ate two a day with black coffee. After a week the jelly dried up and her husband said the white powder started cracking. He wouldn't have to worry about that this week. Edith ate two more sweet rolls in time with the turning bus wheels. The fat woman was still staring at Edith's bag as if she understood what Edith was doing. But she couldn't possibly understand. Edith assured herself that she was only eating to save her husband. She was certainly not eating because she was hungry.

She swallowed hard; she had almost choked on the sixth jelly roll. She had stopped paying full attention to what she was doing. She had begun to think hard about the fat woman. She hoped that the woman did not assume they suffered from the same illness. Edith was positive that she had nothing in common with that woman. Their kind ate to save themselves, but Edith was eating to save her family. There was a huge difference. She had only four rolls left; she was going to miss all that white powder floating down in front of her. She had almost forgotten where she was; she'd actually begun to float like when the dentist filled her up with gas. Edith knew she was not quite in control of her faculties, but that didn't matter anymore. She felt good. She had no idea red sweet jelly rolls made you feel so lightheaded.

Her whole body was jumping. Instead of feeling heavy and full, she had those female twitches between her legs. Her thighs pushed into each other; she felt her whole body puffing up like a fresh hot roll coming straight from the oven to the table. Just as Edith pictured the baker filling the roll with all that sweet red jelly, she gave out a bigger groan than she'd ever remembered giving out while lying right next to her very own man. Her thighs were calming down. She almost hated to let go of all that sweetness between her legs. But she'd finished the last jelly roll; there was no more white powder blocking her vision. Quickly Edith commanded her legs to relax. She looked down at her feet just to make sure her Thom McAns were still there. Then she pulled her dress down as far over her knees as it would go.

The fat woman's head was nodding to the same beat as Edith's head. Edith looked at where the woman's thighs ought to be; she panicked. She couldn't make out two thighs in all that slumped-over body. But she wasn't exactly looking for thighs; she was more looking for why their heads were nodding together at the exact same time. The fat woman seemed to be feeling real good. As if she felt what Edith had just been feeling when she finished off the last jelly roll to save her family. Then Edith did it; she couldn't stop herself. She locked her own green-hazel eyes straight onto the fat woman. Then her vision cleared, clearer than it had been all day. The fat woman had got what she wanted.

She was nodding her head slowly, pushing something from her head directly into Edith Jeanne Drinkwater's.

Edith had no choice but to accept what the woman was giving her; she had locked their eyes together. Besides she had been waiting her whole life for a single moment of truth. She'd always known she was capable of visions sent by the Lord, only Edith never expected to receive from a fat woman riding on a moving bus. Here they were, taking up the whole front row including the aisle; it was unavoidable. That was the way her mother said the Lord always worked — He was unavoidable whenever you most wanted to be avoided. Edith decided to act with courage. If this was her moment, she was going to receive and be hallowed. Only it was too bad she had come to peace through the fat woman's eyes. Edith decided to prepare herself. She quit thinking altogether and opened her eyes as wide as she possibly could.

She shook her head, shaking out what the Lord was sending in. She was seeing herself staring out at her from the fat woman's eyes. Only it wasn't exactly Edith. It was, as far as she could tell, Edith — a wee bit deformed. She was still five feet one-and-a-half inches tall and her arms were still short and slender, but her stomach had been pulled way out of shape. In the eyes of that woman Edith was fat, so fat that her stomach took up both of the woman's eyes. Edith was horrified; she had never seen such a big stomach before. She was not at all clear that this was what the Lord Jesus had wanted her to see when she gave her eyes to the fat woman.

Her stomach grumbled; the picture was making her ill. She thought for a moment that if she could just open the moving bus window, she could throw up all fourteen jelly rolls into the street and let the bus roll right over them, killing the red jelly out flat. Then she could forget everything. But Edith knew that was impossible. She'd swallowed hard every single bite of those sweet red rolls; she'd taken them in as if in preparation for her single moment of truth.

Edith was still staring at herself in the fat woman's eyes when she noticed her neck had disappeared into her stomach. All of a sudden she saw one head after another rise up out of the stomach and take over. There must be some mistake. The heads had begun to look like her mother's and her mother's sister's heads. It was horrible; the fat woman was gulping down all the women Edith had ever known. Finally, Edith's own head came back. She smiled out at herself, only the smile seemed far away. She forced her eyes to focus. The smile was hiding under a thick veil and Edith was wearing a blue bonnet. She was becoming that woman. They all were becoming one giant fat woman. Edith began to think that inside every thin woman was a fat woman waiting to get out.

Edith took her eyes back. What if all the other passengers had seen what just happened to her? She sucked her stomach in; nobody was going to call Edith Jeanne Drinkwater fat. Nobody on this bus was going to know what Edith knew. It was okay for Edith to know that all of them — all the women on the bus — were one and the same. But she wasn't going to be the one shouting out the new gospel, even if the vision had come her way first. She reminded herself that she'd never been one for leadership; she had no ability there. She could follow though, without losing a single step. Edith made a decision to walk off the bus as if nothing had happened. As if nothing concerning the order of things had changed. She was going to hold her stomach in for the rest of her life, just to make sure no one guessed the truth. Oh, she'd come around once the others did. But not until then; she was going to keep it all to herself just as her mother had done with her. She would not point out that blue bonnet to her daughter after all. Edith was going to keep silent and keep her stomach in.

When the bus finally stopped moving, it stopped where it always did. She was glad for that. At least some things never changed. The bus stopped, even with the flagpole which was right across the street from Young's Coffee Shop. The fat woman stood up at the same time Edith did. In fact, they almost bumped into each other stepping into the aisle. Edith couldn't wave to her daughter who she knew was standing right in front of the flagpole. She was too busy trying to avoid connecting with the fat woman. But she saw she needn't worry. The woman was holding back, letting Edith go first. That was the polite thing to do, she told herself. Those people had to learn to wait their turn. Edith choked on the end of that thought.

When the driver opened the doors of the bus, Edith felt like her own stomach was opening up. The doors opened straight down the middle. She could breathe again. Her left Thom McAn led her into the aisle. There still seemed to be some confusion as to who was going out first. She thought it had all been decided. So it had. Just as Edith's left foot took the lead, the woman opened her mouth, "You go first, honey. I'm in no hurry. Besides, it doesn't matter anyway." Edith wanted to stop right in the middle of the aisle, turn around and head straight back to her seat. But she'd already put both feet on the ground and the fat woman was right behind her, putting down her own two feet on the very same ground.

O

Miss Ohio

Tonight she will pick the winner. Closing her eyes, she imagines fifty red satin sashes in one long, single curving line. Most of the sashes don't lie flat, in between the right and left breast. But her mother says a good-fitting sash lies completely flat, no matter what sits underneath. So she waits for the moment the camera stops briefly on the sash that fits completely flat. That moment could come at any time. In order to pick the real Miss America, she tells herself to remain alert. Then she'll stand up — ahead of time — to make her announcement. Afterwards she'll go to bed — confident she picked correctly. In the morning she'll wake up feeling like a winner herself.

She is upstairs in her parents' pale blue bedroom, propping up four big foam-rubber pillows on the floor against the end of the king-size bed. She turns the lights on and off. The overhead light is very bright and makes one big shadow on the carpet at the end of the bed. She turns to dim her mother's night light on the right-hand side of the king-size bed. Dim is perfect for pageant viewing. She can see the TV, the girls inside, and Roger, the son of her mother's best friend Phyllis, who always sits next to her.

Lying down on the carpet — on her side of the pillows — she waits for Roger, who is making popcorn in her father's popcorn machine. Roger takes a long time in the kitchen, longer than her father takes. And salt. Her father knows exactly how much salt she likes. With Roger if she wants salt she must go downstairs, pull out the chair from the kitchen table, lean it next to the counter without scratching it and climb up on the chair to reach the cabinet where her mother keeps the saltshaker. Then she must turn the saltshaker upside down, shake three times and stir the popcorn with a big wooden spoon. She hopes Roger will hurry. The dance routines are next; she doesn't want to miss a single routine.

She remembers — five months ago — the first time Roger came to babysit. She is almost nine years old. Roger is fourteen. Neither of them is happy about spending Saturday evenings together. They don't go to the same school or have the same friends. She likes to talk. Roger wants to watch TV. She has her favorite shows, but she has other interests too. Mostly, she wants company. Someone to play with, talk a few things over together, maybe — around eight o'clock — have walnut cream cheese and raspberry jelly sandwiches with potato chips crumbled into the walnut cream cheese. Once in a while she likes to put the lights on *very dim* like her parents do, to listen to a piano and violin sonata on the radio. But she'd give up a radio concert in exchange for a little conversation, only exchanges are not acceptable to Roger. So they settle into a routine which she finds boring. Aunt Lou's All Natural Popping Corn, TV until ten o'clock, then bed.

The first dance routines begin. It's always some version of "The Stars and Stripes Forever." The song doesn't mean anything to her even though her father says it's patriotic. She sits in the middle of the foam rubber pillows, watching the red sashes with gold lettering move across the screen. The girls from the south are in the front row. The M.C., Mr. Monty Hall from "Let's Make A Deal," calls them "our southern-most beauties." The audience applauds. She doesn't like the nicknames that Mr. Monty Hall gives the fifty states. "Girl" is bad enough. Once she overheard her mother telling her father that no one is a girl after her first period. He must stop calling the secretaries in his office "girl." They are all women. According to her mother's definition, she has two more years until she will be a woman. It happens overnight, her mother says; a girl gets her period and becomes a woman forever.

It's almost nine. There is only one more hour until she has to pick the winner and go to bed — unless she convinces Roger to let her stay up later. She hears Roger walk into her parents' bedroom before she sees him out of the corner of her eye. Without saying a word, he hands her a bowl of popcorn. She sees that no salt has been added. But, just in case he has surprised her by dumping all the salt into the bottom, she shakes the bowl twice — then sticks a handful in her mouth. No salt. Roger is busy eating his own popcorn from the bowl her father always gives her. He is staring at the TV and talking to her, saying something about exchanges. He might be interested in an exchange tonight.

After getting some salt, she rushes back upstairs hoping Roger hasn't changed the channel to "Hawaii Five-O." He tells her to move over, even before she finishes arranging herself on the carpet in front of the TV. The contestants are busy changing into designer swimsuits which come in three styles: spaghetti strap, low back or V-neck. Mr. Monty Hall says all the girls are winners as far as he is concerned. Then he announces the semifinalists. Three of her choices — Miss Hawaii, Miss Texas and Miss New York — are also included in the official selection. Their red sashes lie almost flat across their breasts. From her stretched out position in front of the TV, she sits up. Her back straightens against the foam rubber pillows and she concentrates all her attention on picking the winner. Roger is talking to her. He definitely wants to make an exchange tonight. He wants her to be Miss Ohio, their home state. He will be the M.C., Mr. Roger Miller. They will have their own competition. She can stay up at least another half hour, until ten-thirty. The talent show is beginning. Roger wants the two of them to start their competition right away. "Stand up," he says, "in front of the TV." When Miss Hawaii dances, he tells her she must dance too.

Dancing is something she loves. She is taking Dances From India — with live music — at Meadowbrook Elementary school. Learning to move one part of her body while not moving the other part is hard for her. She likes to move and shake everything at once. But she is discovering how to make a circle with her head and her stomach without moving her shoulders or her arms. Miss Wada says to listen carefully to the sound of the reed flute. She loves the slow quiet melody and reminds herself that Indian flutes are made from trees instead of silver or gold.

Miss Hawaii is introduced while Roger introduces her. He announces that Miss Ohio will begin her dance. Roger wants her to take off her robe, so she can dance better. He says to call him Mr. Roger Miller. Before she finishes her popcorn she stands up to dance without her robe. She listens to Miss Hawaii's music. It's faster than the Indian flute music, but she thinks she can keep up. She dances right next to Miss Hawaii, imagining their hips moving in the same direction. She is surprised. This is the first time Roger wants to play a game. He says they are improvising, making their own competition.

Roger says Miss Hawaii is moving her right shoulder slowly, then her left shoulder and making small circles with her knees. So she tries moving her right shoulder first then her left shoulder while her own knees begin making small circles. Mr. Roger Miller is sitting up, staring at her. He says that Miss Hawaii is moving her head to the rhythm. She tries not to laugh at herself. This is the first time she has ever imitated a future Miss America. Roger's pale face is starting to have some color.

A light red flush fills his cheeks, then his whole forehead turns bright red. The TV audience applauds. Mr. Roger Miller applauds. She bows low from the waist like Miss Wada teaches the class. Slowly, a little at a time — bend the head, the shoulders; the arms will follow. The waist, the hips, then bend the knees slightly. The entire class bends together to the last long notes of the reed flute.

When both she and Miss Hawaii finish their dances, Roger says it's time for the examination. He explains that all the contestants are examined during the commercials by specialists, doctors who examine each girl just in case she is sick and won't be able to travel during her year as Miss America. Roger tells her to lie down on the carpet; he will prop up her head with the foam rubber pillows. He wants to start the examination right away — it's late, way past her bed time. She has never heard about the examinations. She isn't sure she wants to be examined even if she gets to be Miss Ohio. Besides, she can't see the parade of evening gowns if she's lying on the carpet with her head propped up. Roger is busy arranging the pillows, giving her directions, folding and unfolding his hands. Roger tells her to lie down and act like Miss Ohio or go to bed. He talks to her like she really is Miss Ohio. He asks her to describe how she will bring peace to the planet and what she will do with the prize money. She plays right along because she likes answering questions. This is the most conversation she and Roger have ever had together.

Roger's face is red. He is touching her forehead and asking more questions. *What does it mean to be Miss America? Is her family proud of her? How does it feel to be so beautiful?* Mr. Roger Miller uses both hands to examine Miss Ohio while the audience applauds the parade of evening gowns. The sound on the TV is very loud. She feels a hand rubbing her stomach the way her mother does whenever she has a stomachache. Her right leg starts to itch. Then she sees her legs slowly opening into a big wide V. She watches as a pair of hands — fingers — run up and down her legs. She doesn't like being tickled. But she isn't being tickled. Roger is acting very serious and talking like he is a real doctor. He tells her to lie still. The examination is only half over. She doesn't feel like herself. She thinks she should get up and go to bed. She hears the semifinalists answering their questions. She tries to keep her eyes open. The harder she tries to open her eyes the more they shut tight. She doesn't move. Her pajama top is lifted up. Cold, wet hands pull down her cotton bottoms. She wishes she could stand up, walk right inside the TV, put on a red sash and stand in line with Miss Hawaii, Miss Texas and Miss New York.

Roger lowers his voice. He whispers into her ear. She can't hear anything. She feels a tongue licking her ear. One wet hand rubs her chest where her breasts are starting to grow. She can't move. She opens her eyes long enough to see Roger's other hand touching the space between her legs that her mother calls a vagina. She sees his hand moving — slow at first, in small circles, then faster and faster.

She starts to feel weightless and to perspire all at the same time. She stops trying to open her eyes. Her whole body feels like it's growing two, three inches longer, right there on the carpet in her parents' bedroom, in front of their king-size bed. She imagines herself turning into Miss Ohio, with a smooth, red satin sash lying flat across her growing breasts.

After a few minutes, she isn't sure where Roger's hands are but she's not going to open her eyes to find out; she's feeling too good. She feels like this — in the bathtub — when her mother soaks her clean from head to foot. They take a bath together whenever they play goldfish in a glass bowl. First they pour water over each other with her yellow plastic drinking cup. Then her mother rubs her head with the warm soapy, soft pink washcloth, dripping water all the way down her shoulders and her chest. They make goldfish tails out of their legs that look just like the letter V in the alphabet. Then her mother washes her goldfish tail, starting with her baby toes and moving slowly up the sides of her tail which are her thighs, to the hole between her legs that her mother calls a vagina. They both giggle so hard that she swallows some of the soapy water and has to get out of the tub before she washes her mother's goldfish tail.

Whenever her mother moves the pink washcloth up close to the letter V she feels her legs grow longer, while her body becomes weightless just like now. She never says anything to her mother. But after she washes the soap out of her eyes, she sees her mother smiling. Roger is breathing so loud she can barely hear the TV. She's afraid she will miss the next announcement — the finalists. Roger says the examination is almost over; he thinks he picked a winner himself. The new Miss Ohio. She feels his hands moving all around her goldfish tail. Over and over again on the same place her mother cleans with the soapy, soft pink washcloth.

She hears voices. Roger is talking to her, telling her to make lots of noise; she doesn't have to be quiet. She giggles like playing goldfish in a glass bowl with her mother. This time she hears herself laughing out loud. She's doing fine, Roger says. Only she isn't doing anything but lying on the carpet in her parents' bedroom being examined by Mr. Roger Miller. She thinks about not being a goldfish in a bowl anymore but still feeling weightless. She knows that goldfish can't live outside the glass bowl. Then her whole body shudders, like a dying goldfish, only she isn't dying, she's leaping out of the water, out of the clear glass bowl and gasping for breath.

Mr. Roger Miller is shaking her hand and calling her a winner. Maybe they can play again, he says, next Saturday. She looks at the TV. Miss New York is walking down the long promenade, with a silver crown on her head, only she's not smiling. She doesn't even look happy. Her red sash lies completely flat across her chest but she's crying. Miss New York returns to center stage, bows low, once to the right then once to the left.

She wants to announce that she cannot play goldfish in a glass bowl with her mother anymore. She's not completely sure why, but after tonight she doesn't think playing goldfish with her mother will be half as much fun as it used to be. Roger is making his own announcement. Stand up, he says, the new Miss Ohio deserves a round of applause. She stands up, bending low from the waist like Miss Wada teaches the class. Slowly, a little at a time, bend the head, the shoulders, the arms will follow. She starts to cry. The waist, the hips, then bend the knees slightly. She is crying as she watches Miss New York blow the audience a kiss good-bye.

O

Hot Chicken Wings

Esther wanted silence. It had been eight hours since she had met Channah and Saul in the AIR FLORIDA terminal for their flight to Jamaica, and Esther was afraid she wasn't going to last the whole ten days. She had waited months for this reconciliation. But growing inside her was the terrible feeling that she needed to be saved from her very own parents. Then she laughed out loud. Maybe it was really Channah and Saul who needed to be saved from her, their very own daughter.

Esther took the elevator down to the lobby of the Windsor Hotel. Walking out the back door, she found herself in the middle of a pink patio, hot-pink lounge chairs everywhere. Nothing was familiar. She was used to the Piccolo Porch, to all the Jews sitting in brown wicker chairs at the Doral Hotel in Miami Beach, reading the *Jewish Daily Forward* and arguing about Polish solidarity.

The sun reflected a glaring light on the patio, but Esther couldn't stop staring at the pink plush. Her white cheeks burned.

She had to close her eyes. With her eyes shut tight Esther's mind snapped into focus and she understood the problem with the pink. It just wasn't real. Staying here, right in front of the ocean, with the cool breeze coming in off the water, piped-in reggae music, fried plantain and tropical drinks served all day poolside definitely made her a tourist.

But Channah said they should try some place new, different; to give the family another chance, Esther hoped. They could never have reconciled in Miami Beach. There were too many relatives and family friends wanting to know what's what all the time. So they had come to Jamaica.

Esther's family on her mother's side were descendants of Sephardic Jews who had settled in Montego Bay when the Jews were expelled from Spain. As she grew up Esther learned that the Caribbean had always been a haven for Jews, sometimes the only place that would take them in.

She knew her parents rarely travelled outside the U.S.; neither her father nor her mother felt safe anywhere the Jews had been expelled or exterminated. To date, Channah and Saul had been to Israel, the Anne Frank house in Amsterdam and Miami Beach. It had been a risk to fly to Jamaica, but her mother felt as though the family were returning home. So, okay, maybe she was only half a tourist.

"Hello, darlin. Welcome to Jamaica." Quickly Esther turned away from the hot-pink lounge chairs and opened her eyes.

"Charlotte Loudon, here." Charlotte was smiling a huge smile. Esther tried to smile back. She reached instead for the Jewish star hanging between her breasts.

"Esther Pearl Friedman. I'm with my parents, we came here to talk."

Charlotte wasn't just smiling. She was grinning from behind her eyes. But Esther could barely meet her smile, even though it was the smile itself she craved. Charlotte was dressed in a uniform. A green military blouse covered her large round breasts. She wore a tight, khaki colored skirt, short above the knees, with black ankle socks and black tie shoes.

"Are you the tour guide?"

"Man, I guard di door rite here at di Windsor Hotel." The woman was laughing in Esther's face.

Esther thought fast. She knew she couldn't spend all ten days with her parents, no matter how much she'd missed them over the last seven months. She took a deep breath before pleading softly. "I want to travel with you."

"Dat okay wid me, honey. When yuh want see mi beautiful country?"

"As soon as possible, I mean it... and Charlotte..." Esther swallowed hard before whispering into the big smile, "I go with girls."

"Girls fine wid me, mi luv." The guard reached out for Esther's hand. She had a firm grip. "Check me later, darlin. Ah be waitin."

"Esther!" Channah walked out into the pink patio just as Esther's hand met the hand of the woman in the khaki colored skirt who was already turning around, walking towards the hotel lobby.

"Who was that?" Channah wanted to know.

"My tour guide."

"Esther Friedman, you don't need a tour guide in Montego Bay. We came here for the sun. To say *Kaddish* for our family. And to talk."

"I need a tour guide wherever I am." Esther needed patience. It had only been a year since she had told her parents the wonderful news that she loved women. "I'll meet you for dinner — just tell me what time." Esther understood her parents' disappointment. Not one of their three daughters had turned out according to the family plan. Her parents felt they deserved better than a divorce from an assimilated French Jew and a marriage to a Freudian psychiatrist who didn't believe in standing under the *chupah*. The problem was that her parents didn't understand Esther's disappointment with them.

"Seven o'clock, sharp. We'll wait for you in the lobby." Esther tried to meet her mother's eyes, but when she did, all she saw was the flash of her mother's pain moving across her face. She wanted to hug Channah, to tell her she was glad they came to some place new. But she was afraid Channah wouldn't hug her back. Instead she nodded, turned around and walked back into the hotel, wondering which door Charlotte was guarding now.

Esther stood alone in front of the elevators. When the doors opened, Charlotte walked out, almost bumping into Esther.

"Estie, where yuh been keepin yuh sweet self?" The gold in Charlotte's teeth caught her eyes.

"When does the tour begin?"

"Tomorrow mi day off." Charlotte's whole body smiled when she spoke. Her feet tapped the hotel floor lightly. Esther felt the smile coming up through the earth itself. By tapping her foot, Charlotte returned what she borrowed. "Why yuh head so busy, man?"

"I was just watching you live." Esther winked at Charlotte. "So tomorrow's our day. What'll we do?"

"Whatever yuh want, sweet Estie. Mi coming early, so we have di whole day."

"I want to eat Jamaican." Esther decided to take advantage of vacationing — for the first time in her life — beyond the brown wicker chairs of Miami Beach.

"Sure darlin, Ah go cook. Wear yuh walkin shoes. We walkin far to mi house from di bus. Catch yuh later, dis hotel need a guard." After a quick nod goodbye, Charlotte walked away.

Alone in the elevator, Esther tried to understand what she wanted from this trip. She knew she had longed for her family. But she didn't miss the heartache that always followed being together as family, as Jews. Even studying at Brandeis where most of the students were Jews and she was majoring in Judaic Studies, hadn't brought back that warm feeling of belonging to her people. Crowds of heterosexual Jews made her feel worse.

It was only Sunday. She told herself to take one day at a time, hour by hour if she had to.

At seven sharp Esther met her parents in the hotel lobby. They walked towards her just like two ordinary human beings. Everyone had dressed for the evening. Channah had on her favorite skirt-and-blouse ensemble. Esther had to admit her mother had good taste; the material was a soft silk, light blue and sea green. Channah's face was already tanned. Saul wore his summer suit, without a tie. He smiled at Esther.

"Where are we going for dinner?" Esther's voice was friendly.

"The Montego Bay Beach and Tennis Club, it's just up the road and comes highly recommended in the *Kosher Traveler*," Channah answered, not looking at Esther and not looking away, just looking.

Channah and Saul walked out the Windsor in front of Esther. They formed a perfect triangle. Esther remembered her therapist always said to stay away from triangles, only Esther had thought she meant love triangles, but now she knew that any triangle was dangerous, and that there was no way out, but physically to step out. Besides, a triangle was only half a Jewish star.

Saul asked the bellman to get a cab. Esther felt a large movement behind her. Charlotte.

"Yuh parents dese, sweet darlin?" Esther reeled around, hostile, until she realized no one had heard the love talk but Esther and Charlotte. Esther coughed.

"These are my parents, Saul and Channah Friedman." She knew her mother expected to be introduced.

"You're Esther's new friend, aren't you?" Channah said. Charlotte grinned. Esther didn't say a word.

"Cab's here." Saul called out. Charlotte walked with them.

For a minute Esther imagined she was going to bend down and step right into the cab with her parents. But she didn't.

The cab pulled up at a giant ranch. As soon as they walked into the dining room, which was like an old cowboy movie — big round tables in huge circles circling a gigantic fireplace — Esther knew her mother was going to say that the dining room was a little too much. Saul looked around before making his announcement, "Not many of us in here."

"That's exactly what I was thinking." Channah looked at Esther for support. Esther knew her parents were uncomfortable in the strange *goyishe* dining room and so was she.

Esther wondered about her mother's relatives; they had all been small shopkeepers and members of the United Congregation of Israelites. She couldn't picture anyone in her family sitting down to eat in a place like this. She wished her relatives were still alive so she could talk to them about being outsiders in beautiful Jamaica. Esther looked at her parents; she knew they longed for the *Jewish Daily Forward* and Miami Beach, where everybody drank iced tea from short, wide rimmed glasses and played bridge for hours. For a moment, they were a family again.

But Esther couldn't stop thinking about Charlotte. Where was she? What was she having for dinner? Was she with her lover?...Esther closed her eyes to see better: she felt the warmth of two big women sprawled out on a tiny double bed, feeding each other and laughing as the food spilled onto the sheets. Esther decided to have the fresh local tuna. She had read in *National Geographic* that it was a Jamaican fish.

She knew that tuna was *kosher*; the mothers didn't eat their young or prey off other fish. Esther had always hated the image of a mother eating her children. Whenever she smelled *treyf* she immediately saw the floor of the ocean in her head. She pictured big shrimps, scallops, and giant oysters devouring their babies and any other fish swimming in their path.

Keeping kosher had always been important to Esther. When she was thirteen, right after her *Bat Mitzvah,* Esther had immersed herself in the meaning of *kashrut*, in hallowing the very act of eating. It was a way for Esther to eat with Jews everywhere and have Jews everywhere eat at her table.

She closed her eyes, wishing that she was alone with Charlotte. Esther hadn't remembered how depressing it was to be with her parents. She had always wanted an adult relationship with Saul and Channah. *Well, here it is,* she told herself. Then she had to put her fork down and stop eating. "I'm going to the bathroom, the waiter can take my plate."

She looked at herself in the mirror, shaking her head, not wanting to believe that absolutely nothing had changed. She knew her parents were unhappy. They had told no one, not even Rabbi Jacobson that their baby wanted their blessing to bring home a Sabbath bride instead of a groom. So no one had brought up her life; no one had even asked her if she was happy.

Being a lesbian made life with Channah and Saul so difficult. Her mother had stopped inviting her home for the holidays, and Saul had specifically said they weren't interested in any details, not even Esther's new friends. She could still hear Channah's reaction to her good news: *But why did you have to go and spoil everything? Why tell us?* Esther knew then, that the only way into the Friedman family was to be like Channah and Saul. There really wasn't anything to talk about. Esther returned to the table. She looked straight at her parents for the first time since arriving on the island. "I want dessert. Is anyone going to join me?"

"We'll split something with you," Channah said.

"No, I want my own." Esther shut her eyes and waited. Nothing happened. When the waiter came back she ordered Baked Alaska because she had always loved the taste of the meringue on her tongue as it melted.

Saul paid the bill while Esther took a last look at the big round tables. She was back at Camp Ramah, sitting with hundreds of young campers, cutting their *kosher Shabes* chicken breasts simultaneously. She stood to bless the wine, surrounded by over two hundred and fifty adolescent Jewish voices, singing as though their voices alone could call the prophet Elijah back to Earth. That was the last time Esther really felt at home.

Of course it never happened that the entire Camp Ramah dining room began eating at the exact same moment, but Esther used to fantasize every *Shabes*, that all her people everywhere, were striking matches as the sun set, welcoming in the weekly festival. In her mind for one brief moment, she had brought peace to the Jews, and to her family. Finally, Esther had to admit that being Jewish and being a Friedman weren't the same thing.

"Estie, Estie!" Charlotte was waving her hands and calling to Esther. But it didn't look like Charlotte at all. Her green military blouse and khaki colored skirt were gone. Instead, she wore a purple beret balanced just above her left eyebrow. Deep red rouge was smoothed into brown skin; red lip gloss wet her mouth. Charlotte had hooped gold earrings, two and three, in each ear.

"Ya *finally* ready, man?" Esther nodded, following her out the lobby of the Windsor Hotel and down the road to the bus stop. In the hot sun, Charlotte's black pants shined and her white blouse looked like silk. She carried a red and green, hand-woven pouch and a small, brown paper bag in her left hand.

Charlotte's legs moved fast on the gravel road. Esther had to run to keep up. This was a new Charlotte, quick, taking up space. On the bus, Charlotte sat down, stretched her legs out across an entire seat, and said hello whenever someone she knew walked by. Esther sat alone in the row directly behind Charlotte.

By the time they reached downtown, Charlotte was asleep and Esther's eyes were wide open. The bus stopped inside a huge open market decorated in banners of gold, green, shiny black and red. In booth after booth people sold food, clothes, records. The smells — red onions, ripe mango, salt fish — blended together, making Esther sick. Charlotte woke up and motioned for Esther to follow her.

They walked across the street to another bus stop, and waited ten minutes. They sat again in separate rows, as if they knew, without speaking that both of them needed a lot of space before their afternoon together. Pulling against the force of gravity, the bus climbed straight up into the Jamaican hills, while the town below got smaller and smaller.

Skinny, bone-thin dogs ran everywhere; the driver kept his hand on the horn. A baby lay crying right in the middle of the road, sprawled out on all fours, trying to crawl to the other side. The bus circled around the screaming infant. As the bus climbed up, the temperature rose inside. Esther was hot. Everywhere there were trees, large wide-leafed palm trees reaching out, shielding the villages and the people.

"Green, all shades; Jamaica was divided into shades of dark, light and yellow greens. From the window, the Jamaican green reminded Esther of Israel; slowly, she let in the yellow green Jamaican hillside. But she heard her father's voice in her head, like a tape recorded message playing over and over again: *Israel is the most beautiful country in the whole world.*

"Okay, Estie. Me stop dis." Charlotte hadn't spoken for at least twenty minutes; Esther didn't recognize her voice, but she felt them rise in unison, a pair of woman-bodies bending and rising together in dance. "Ready for some walkin?" Charlotte looked at Esther for the first time since picking her up at the Windsor.

"What's in your bag?" Esther asked.

"Our supper, man. I went to di butcher dis morning for some chicken, wings and legs." Charlotte was impatient. Esther didn't say a word; how could she explain the laws of *kashrut* to Charlotte?

Even though she wanted to eat Jamaican, she hadn't planned to eat *treyf*. She never ate meat in restaurants unless it had been ritually slaughtered and blessed. Out of respect for her people, and for the food itself, Esther separated the *kosher* from the un*kosher,* the holy from the unholy, and ate only what was permitted by Jewish law. When she ate, Esther belonged to Jerusalem.

"Mi children waitin.... Estie, pick up yuh feet."

"Kids?"

"Yah man, mi have children, one boy and two pretty pretty little girls, brown and pretty." Esther didn't think she heard right; this was the first time Charlotte had said anything about kids.

"Charlotte, you got a husband?"

Charlotte nodded, her purple beret moved up and down. They walked side by side now; their buttocks moving from right to left, hitting each other slightly because they were walking up hill while their bodies pulled them down. "Mi man come and go; him workin in Miami Beach most time. Him send me a letter before him come home."

"What about your woman?" Esther concentrated on walking straight up hill. Charlotte didn't owe her any explanations. For a second, Esther wondered if Charlotte's husband worked at the the Doral Hotel in Miami Beach; she couldn't bring herself to ask.

"Oh yes, darlin, when mi man travelling, mi and mi woman Caroline go to bed and have we a sweet time. Sometimes we don't get up for a whole day, just to feed the children and den we meet again." They were almost at the top of the hill.

"Mi man love me, Estie. Mi have his picture at mi home. You'll see, girl." Charlotte pointed to a path off the dirt road. They headed straight down the side of the hill, into the overgrown weeds, bushes and very green trees.

Holding back a big yellow-green bush, Charlotte showed Esther where to walk. As she moved forward, the same odor Esther always smelled on her body whenever she was afraid came up to her nose. The path wasn't cleared well and the brush scratched her legs. They climbed down, deep into the underbrush; the deeper they went, the greener the leaves became, the stronger Esther's body smelled.

Looking up, she saw that Charlotte had taken them way off the main dirt road. They stood in the middle of a row of small wooden huts. Walking over to the far end, they stopped in front of a silver tin door. Esther heard voices. Out of the bushes came a young boy as Charlotte whistled long and slow.

"Where di rest of di children?" Charlotte bent down to the size of her son, whispering and kissing inside each of his ears. Dem wid Caroline?" The boy nodded, standing almost at attention, watching Esther. His mother's eyes were in him.

"Let we go." Charlotte nodded towards the door.

The hut was a single room, as big as her Windsor closet and bathroom combined. In the center of the room was a double bed; Charlotte sat herself at the head. The boy jumped up, circling his mother with his body, protecting her. Esther stood in the doorway taking in all the Jamaican landscape never mentioned in the travel brochures.

To the right of the entrance was a big dresser with a mirror attached. Next to the dresser were several plastic milk cartons piled one on top of the other. From where she stood Esther could see dishes and silverware arranged in neat rows inside the milk cartons. On top of the cartons was a double gas burner. Everywhere, clothes were folded into neat piles.

The floor of Charlotte's house was made of firmly packed brown dirt. A broom was in the left corner by the doorway, and a dust pan. The only window was on the wall opposite the bed. The frame was empty, but the green from outside grew up around the glassless hole, filling it with a thick green softness.

"Estie, si-down, yuh rude girl; dis mi home."

Charlotte cooked. She poured water from a jug on the floor into a sauce pan and added a cup of uncooked rice. She made a work space on the bed by propping up a six by twelve wooden board with two bricks at each end. Taking the chicken parts out of the bag she had carried since early that morning, she separated the legs from the wings, making two piles, dipping and rolling each piece into a flour mixture. After flouring each piece,

Charlotte covered the chicken with spices. Esther watched, trying to figure out what the great rabbis would tell her about eating Charlotte's unclean food.

Charlotte lit the burner. She poured oil into a frying pan, waited a few minutes, watching the oil sizzle and get hot. Then one by one, she placed the wings into the hot pan, stopping for only a second to stir the rice. Every few minutes she added spices, red, black and green powders to the hot oil. When she was done frying the wings, she started over with the legs. Charlotte's love went straight into the frying pan and into the steaming rice.

On the edge of the bed, Charlotte spread out a single straw mat painted red, filled one plate with hot rice and fried chicken wings then put it on the mat in front of Esther. "Eat."

"I don't want to eat alone."

"Where yuh manners, girl? Jus eat."

Esther picked up the fork. What did it mean that she was about to eat Jamaican chicken wings and rice? She reminded herself that she had arranged this day, she had made the date with Charlotte and even told her she wanted to eat Jamaican. So Esther put some rice on the end of her fork, added a piece of chicken and brought the fork slowly up to her mouth. She was eating Charlotte's wings, *treyf* and unclean that they were.

The food had lost its heat, but when Esther put it in her mouth, she tasted all the Jamaican spices that Charlotte had added while she cooked. Spices Esther couldn't see by looking at the cooked food. She had to taste them to know that they were actually red hot and sweet all in the same bite. Like nothing she had ever tasted before.

Esther chewed. The spices were overpowering. This wasn't the first time that Esther had ever eaten *treyf,* but in the past, whenever she brought unclean food to her lips, she had never been able to enjoy it as she did now. She remembered the first time she made love to a woman. That was the beginning. Esther had been afraid to bring her tongue down between Judith's legs. She had spent a long time kissing arms, shoulders, eyes and face.

Finally there was nothing left to do but bring her wet tongue straight down Judith's breasts, stomach and inside her thighs. Those first woman smells had been overpowering too, sweet and hot like Jamaican spices. When her tongue circled between Judith's small thighs, Esther told herself to open her eyes and look at the curly mound of dark, black hair protecting her lover's vagina, but she had been afraid to look.

"Tasting is the same as looking," Judith had said, reaching down to hold Esther's head close to her body. Esther had known she was right, so she let herself breathe in a little at a time, all the different smells hidden between Judith's legs. She remembered being surprised that the lips outside Judith's vagina had only a faint sweet smell. It was the inside that smelled strong and tasted so wet. Using her fingers to open Judith, Esther had to fight off the pious old Jew in her head. He was tearing apart a red, treyf, steaming lobster. Then slowly, as though praying, he dipped the white sweet, unholy fish into a pool of melted butter.

With her mouth inside Judith, Esther began to chew, taking small, gentle bites. Just as she was crossing over to join her lover, Channah and Saul pushed into her head. They stared at her, *their baby,* and Channah screamed, "Go! Wash yourself until you're clean, don't come into my house with any of that filthy *treyf* on your tongue. Get rid of the smell before you walk into my kitchen." Esther had had to stop, close her mouth before she gagged, and bring her head back up, next to Judith's.

They had held each other while Esther's whole body shook. But she wasn't shaking now. She was taking another bite out of Charlotte's sweet wing and thinking that all her life, she had been afraid of new, unknown and different spices, but now she was chewing bite by bite, Charlotte's crisp Jamaican skin.

"This is good. How do you get the flavors hot and sweet at the same time?" Esther piled more rice on her plate; stuffing her mouth full, she barely took time out to chew and swallow.

"Slow down, girl. Mi knows yuh eat rice before. Yuh eatin like yuh neva eat in yuh whole life." Charlotte shook her head; her son was laughing.

"I feel like I haven't eaten for days, even weeks." She was eating, really eating, almost as if for the first time. She laughed at herself. This then was Charlotte and Esther making love.

"Yuh want see some good pictures? I have one picture of me, mi man and Caroline." Charlotte reached into another pile.

"Sure." Esther talked with her mouth full. They sat on Charlotte's bed, her boy, Esther and Charlotte looking at family pictures. Esther had finished eating and all the kitchen equipment had been pushed aside; they were in the living room now.

"Dis one mi favorite, man. Everybody mi love and who love me be together lookin out at di world." Charlotte handed Esther a picture with three adults standing in the middle of the road. They held each other, looping their arms together behind their backs. Esther knew without asking who was in the picture.

"That's mi woman Caroline, dere at di end, me in di middle and mi man Samuel on di other end." Esther stared at the picture. Something was going on in there that Charlotte wanted her to see.

"Yuh done yet, wid yuh lookin at?"

Esther shook her head. Then she knew; it was in their bodies. If she looked closely at the way they stood, with their hips lightly touching and their thighs and knees bending into each other, Esther saw what Charlotte had been trying to tell her since they met. All three of them — Samuel, Charlotte and Caroline — were lovers. Esther steadied herself on the bed. She needed a few minutes to let in this new piece of truth, because it wasn't just about the three of them, living and loving in Montego Bay.

"So, you're all three together?"

Charlotte nodded.

"Anybody know besides me?"

"Impossible, sweet darlin. In Jamaica a person got to be either-or, Estie, not both. Dem say not enough room in di world for us to be both. But me, hate to choose; me want it all. Yuh di same, dem hungry eyes and dat dancin mouth, tell me right away. That's why mi bring yuh to mi home. Long time, I want someone from outside to talk to. So, I pick up mi sweet Estie." Charlotte reached for the picture.

"I girl, mi separate in mi own beautiful country. Mi whole life, I needin to tell someone. Mi openin doors, lookin around, when I see yuh comin into di Windsor Hotel. I know den, mi found somebody doin what I do."

So Charlotte was alone too, alone in green Jamaica. She had been eating unclean food, separate from her people, for years. Only she was doing just fine. It was Esther who had never learned that eating a little *treyf* was necessary to survive.

Esther had never been free to eat whatever she wanted, because that meant eating alone, without the Jews. Esther had always been afraid to eat by herself; once she started she might never stop. There were too many things to taste, like Charlotte and Caroline and Samuel all at once.

"I've got to leave, Charlotte."

They looked at each other, closing out the boy, the hot chicken wings and rice, and the picture of Charlotte with her two lovers. Esther burned inside. This was only the second time in her whole life that she was full; the first time had been with Judith, her first woman lover. She had been unable to continue loving Judith like she wanted; every time she tried, she imagined her head turning into the red head of a steaming lobster whose antenna reached out to strangle her. But she didn't think that would happen anymore.

"I'll walk yuh to di bus." Charlotte stood up.

They walked then, back up the green path, past all the other huts, and onto the road. When the bus came, Esther climbed the three steps by herself. In the center of the open market where all the smells blended together, Esther walked off the bus. She took a deep breath, slowly breathing in the pungent blend of red onion, ripe mango and salt fish.

O

Voices

1.

Where was I? The mother. Sitting at the kitchen table with my first-born, my oldest daughter, and her teacher from the junior high. Her teacher who was a woman married to a man. A teacher and a woman who wanted my daughter. We sat together at the kitchen table. What did we talk about? The food at the cafeteria. Macaroni on Monday. Egg salad sandwiches, Tuesday. Wednesday, choice of hot dogs or grilled cheese, sliced tomato and dill pickle. When did I know? The truth is I watched it all happen. Right in front of my eyes, at my own kitchen table. A woman thirteen years older than my daughter, wanted my beautiful first-born baby. It's as though the Velveeta melted right into the toasted whole wheat so that I couldn't tell them apart — the bread from the Velveeta. The teacher from the student. A child. The woman loved a child the way I loved my husband. How did I know? I knew I was the mother. That had to count for something. Although for what, I can't say anymore.

I watched *you* become one of them — those women who go with each other instead of doing like the rest of us. Now, seventeen years later and all grown up, you want to know why I didn't do anything. To help. Do anything — what was to do? You're saying it was a hard time. *For you.* What about me? I wasn't so old as to know what to do. There wasn't anyone to talk to and there was your baby sister, my other daughter. What was going to happen with her? I've been over it a thousand times in my head. *Homosexuality.* One of my own. I thought for sure this was just some passing thing. Who would have dreamed that a teacher would carry on like that in front of the girl's own mother. Crushes. I was praying for a crush. Then I decided it was a little more than a crush; you had it on each other. So it was a serious crush. But still. I don't think I saw the whole situation clearly in the beginning. Who could have? I had to forgive myself. It wasn't easy. I imagined calling the whole thing off at the kitchen table.

But *she* was very protective of you. Like *she* was the mother instead of me. Even I got confused. I remember. Clearing my throat to talk to the two of you. Together. I started by saying that things weren't right. Only as soon as I opened my mouth, *she* opened hers and asked if there was any more Coca-Cola. Before I could say a word, she changed her mind. Said she had to go home to make supper for her husband. Then you asked what she was fixing. When she said mashed potatoes with melted butter you were up out of your chair. The both of you were out of the house, on your way to the front seat of her red Chevy wagon. It all happened so fast. I didn't realize you weren't coming back for dinner. I thought if only I had been making mashed potatoes, you would've stayed put, to help mash up those little red russet ones — that always were your favorite. But no, we were having liver and onions, your daddy's favorite.

That's how it was. In front of my face the whole time, yet out beyond my reach. For days I dreamed about wiping up the whole sloppy mess with a double-strength paper dish towel. I liked my kitchen clean. After keeping quiet all these years, I see no reason to keep still any longer, not for a single solitary minute. Since you asked me, why didn't I do anything — what was I supposed to do, exactly? Tell me please. I thought keeping an eye on the two of you in my kitchen was above and beyond the call of a mother's duty. I never had a homosexual home for dinner before. A married one. Let me tell you that. Not a woman who did those things. With my daughter. In the beginning, I have to say I was shocked. No, that's not right. I was in shock. What the hell was that woman doing fooling around with you? That was the question I was about to ask the both of you when the mashed potatoes came up and you were out the door in a flash. Okay. I had some deficiencies in the Mother Department. But that was no reason to go off with that woman. No reason. I want to know. What was she doing with a husband *and* with you on the side?

Before her, you used to be so interested in everything I did. My days. You always wanted to know what I did with my time — how I spent every minute you were separated from me. At Ray's Salon of Beauty. Shopping at Kroger's in the meat department. Or playing pinochle with the girls. We used to be so close. But after her... it was like a cyclone hit your mouth — you didn't say a word. Not even a single hello-how-are-you to the rest of us who still lived in this house. But that woman said you were fine. She was telling me, the mother, that you, my daughter, were fine. That's the way you are, she said, quiet in school, not really outgoing. Well, I have a few things to say to her too. Thank you very much for deflowering my daughter. I'd like to send the woman to jail. Throw the whole book at her. For coming into this house and wrecking this family. Tearing us all apart, from limb-to-limb so that we didn't ever recover. Don't think your daddy didn't know. Or your little baby sister. Everybody whispered in the check-out line at Kroger's. All the neighbors. And their kids.

Seventeen years later you are telling me that you were in trouble, alone; cut off from your friends and us — your family. And that I didn't *do* anything. To help. You have one short memory which I will refresh immediately. We talked, finally, as I recall. You and me. Perhaps you don't remember our conversation because it wasn't as vivid as all those other memories you must have stored up in that brain of yours. I told you that I had had it. We were in your bedroom with the door closed. I told you *this was it;* give the woman up. Stop seeing her. Or I was going to do something. What, you wanted to know, what was I going to do? Then you laughed in my face. You said there was nothing I could do; that you would never stop seeing her; that you were in love. Can you imagine? It was worse than I had thought possible. How could a fifteen-year-old be in love with a woman thirteen years her senior? A woman who was married to a man. I said I would turn her in; that I was going straight to the principal. I wasn't really going to the principal, I was too embarrassed. After all, how would it have looked? Me turning in my own daughter because there was something going on between her and one of the married female junior high teachers. But I had to say something. Things had gone way too far. You said, yelling at me, your mother who was trying to offer what little protection I could, that if I ever turned her in, you would run away and never speak to me or your daddy again. Then you walked out of the room, slammed the door in my face and stepped out of the house. Going back over to see *her*. For dinner, I'm sure.

I sat on the bed and cried. I held myself in my own arms for the longest time. As far as I could tell, you were gone for good. I had tried to regain some control of my precious family; only I had lost. But I was the mother. I tell you, that was one of the most humiliating moments in my life. My daughter, my first-born beauty, chose a homosexual relationship with a married woman who was her teacher, over being part of this family. I have never been the same since. I guess you haven't either. No, neither of us. Or her, I suppose. Only I don't want to think about her. She got what she wanted. Exactly what she wanted. We got the rest. What was left to get, that is.

What was left? Of this family? That's what I used to ask myself. When I knew I couldn't do anything, I decided to put all my attention into your baby sister and your daddy. Only it was too late for your daddy. Something had gone out of him. At first, I thought he'd just lost his appetite. Sometimes, when things at the shop weren't going right, he'd come home not wanting to eat his dinner. I understood. A man has a right to refuse his wife's cooking if he's had a hard day. This was different. He wasn't hungry. For most of the entire week. Then he stopped being hungry for me. Do you know what I'm speaking about? He didn't want me anymore. His own wife. But sex was still in the house. Because you were bringing it in the front door. And the back.

After you took up with her the house never smelled the same, no matter how much lemon-scent Lysol I used on the floors or in the bathroom. There was always the smell. I imagined your daddy smelled it too, only he never said a thing. I had felt powerless before, but this was entirely different. My own husband not wanting me. While my daughter was doing it with her married female public school teacher and coming home afterwards. I thought my head would explode. Now I had two secrets and less people than before to talk to. I was separated from my man, my very own husband, through no choice of my own. All we had left between us was the silence. The silence of knowing what was up with our first-born and not saying a word about it. He had to know. You don't just lose desire for no reason. Since we never talked about it, I have no way of knowing, to this day, what specifically was going on with your daddy. But I was the wife. The mother. So I did know a few things. Up until that time, your daddy and I had done very nicely in the bedroom. We knew each other's likes and dislikes and paid attention to them. Let me say this: you have no idea what was going on with the rest of us. No idea.

Into the end of the first year, of you being with her, your baby sister came home from the junior high, crying her eyes out. I knew it. I had been waiting, only it had taken longer than I expected. "What's a lezzie?" she wanted to know. Then she started crying so hard I found myself crying right along side of her. It felt good. After carrying the whole thing by myself for almost one whole year. Never telling anyone. Finally, there was somebody to cry with. Only she didn't know what she was really crying about. I had to think fast. So I opened a cold bottle of Coca-Cola and let her drink straight from the bottle. I was out of straws — the hospital kind with the necks that bend for easy sipping. "Honey," I said, "tell me what they said to you at the junior high. It'll just be between you and me. We won't tell anybody. Not even your daddy." Then she started crying all over again. And so did I. This was worse than I had imagined. I let her cry and drank the entire Coca-Cola myself.

Just before I swallowed off the whole soda, she opened her mouth. "Some guy two lockers down from mine came over to me during lunch period and whispered into my ear, but loud enough for everybody else to hear, *'Your sister's a lezzie. She does it with all the girls. Know what she does?'* He whispered louder. *'She licks pussy.'* Then all the kids at my table started laughing so I laughed too. But I knew it wasn't funny, even though I didn't know what he was talking about. What's a lezzie?"

There you have it. What would you have said to your baby sister right then? Thinking faster than I was used to thinking, I decided to tell most of the truth. I told your twelve-year-old baby sister that a lezzie was a nickname for girls who hung out with other girls instead of boys. I lied about the rest because it had gotten beyond my control. While you were out having a good time with her, I was home holding your baby sister's hand and hungry for your daddy who had lost his appetite. I simply lied about the rest. Said I never heard those words myself. *Licking pussy.* I can barely say them now. Back then, I didn't say those two words. To anyone. And I don't want to say them today. What was I supposed to do? Tell her everything? I did the best I could. I hope you were enjoying yourself because we were miserable. *Miserable.* But you never noticed. You just kept on like everything was okay. Like you and I never had words. How could you? Didn't you love us anymore?

My heart was torn apart watching the two of you carrying on. I don't care if you were only fifteen. I taught you better than that. I've always wanted to ask you if it was worth it. Did you get what you wanted? From each other? Sure seemed so to me. What did I get for keeping quiet, for all my trouble? Protecting her from prosecution, you from public shame; and providing a safe meeting place around my own kitchen table. Just as you were experiencing your very own firecrackers, mine were going to sleep. For good. Your daddy never did recover his appetite. So what did I get? A long distance AT&T phone call, thanking me for all my support? Or a bouquet of the finest red and pink baby carnations, my favorite. No way. Seventeen years later you are sitting at my kitchen table, telling me you were in trouble. Trouble that you are just finding out about today. I'm sorry if you are having a hard time making friends. Or keeping a steady job. I'm sorry too that you find talking so difficult. But I cannot hear that I did nothing.

Could I ask you something? What was I supposed to do? Tell me please, what was I supposed to do? You were one in three of this family who required my complete attention. I'm telling you, since you did not ask, that this whole family was in trouble. Terrible trouble. Only you were too busy with your spectacular sexual awakening to notice what was going on with us. Your mother, your daddy and your little baby sister. We were all very much in need. But not a living soul knew or cared. Until today. Because this is the first time I have told a living soul. Do you hear me?

I don't understand what you are saying. I have always thought I acted honorably. Bearing my own humiliation in private. Staying with your daddy, remaining your mother and taking care of your baby sister. In the end, I told myself, you were my daughter. If you were a homosexual that was your business, not mine. Now you are saying that you couldn't possibly have been in love. That you were too young; and she was your teacher. What you needed was a coach. Friends. Family. What am I supposed to do with this information? I'd like to know. Because it is coming way too late for me. If you want to apologize for carrying on like you did, that's one thing. But I will not be implicated here. I tried to help in the only way I knew how. Please. Make your peace with that. As I made mine a long time ago.

Alone. Without assistance from your daddy. Or the entire public school system. I cannot hear another word. About her. And you. I already said I was sorry you are hurting. So am I. Hurting. But the story is over. It has got to be. I am the mother. You are the daughter. Please. Can't we keep it that way.

2.

I couldn't believe the way your body moved around the court. I stopped to watch. I had to stop. I couldn't help myself. I saw myself in you. But you didn't know. Did you? Did you have any idea? I wanted to walk right up to you in the middle of class, stand next to you and take your arm back in a graceful, full circle sweep so I could look directly in your eyes and tell you. But I couldn't. I could not move out from among the others. Not now. It wouldn't look right. All I could do was watch and not draw attention to my watching: the way you played the net, met the ball and line drived, always keeping your elbow curved in, close to your strong tight body. You were a skillful dancing warrior hitting on the run with a speeding forehand that sliced the air. Your strength embarrassed me. Did you know? Did you have any idea how much I wanted you? I wanted you. I told myself

*not to look away. Not to be afraid. But there was always fear.
The fear of myself. And the loathing of women like me. We loved
and despised each other. Looked and looked away. From deep
inside our buried desire. We kept our hunger to ourselves even
though the longing was consuming. So half a court away, I held
myself still. My eyes waited for your eyes.*

I need you to understand that I didn't know the difference.
The world of women who went with women was hidden, a big
secret to me. I didn't know the difference between "being out"
or "in." Everybody was in. Marriage was a necessary part of my
college education. I found a husband the way I found a subject
to major in. At the end of my sophomore year, I picked them
both when I had to "declare." I couldn't graduate without an
engagement ring solidly in place on my left fourth finger. I
moved out of the dorm in May, married in June, and left the city
for the suburbs in July. I knew how to coach girls' sports but I
had no idea how to be a wife. After a honeymoon to Niagara
Falls, David and I set up house in a one-bedroom duplex
surrounded by young married couples who were just like us. The
world of women loving women receded into my imagination.
Past relationships became infatuations. I remembered infatua
tions only as crushes. Late-night crushes were slightly flirtatious
moments, diversions from school work and exams. Until I barely
admitted, even to myself who knew better, to anything more than
the way the girls in the dorm gave each other breast examinations. I knew I was *not* one of them just because I had slipped
once and stayed out all night. My survival depended on complete
denial. It was the most appropriate response at the time, if you
loved one of your own.

That fall I started my first full-time job, junior high coach-
ing and teaching physical education. David worked construc-
tion. I had married a real man; strong, secure and completely
heterosexual. Six years later your arm arching in that slow full-
moon serve caught my eye; the edge of the wooden frame sliced
through my vision as I stood half a court away. I had to stop what

I was doing. In that single moment, I knew I was living a lie. But I do not believe I hurt you. That is a lie you are hurting me with now. Back then I couldn't imagine that my life would ever be different. Or that in twelve, thirteen years, homosexuals would march up Fifth Avenue, dancing and giving speeches in the park. All I knew was that I had to have you. I was not interested in being your teacher. I didn't see your age, my husband, or the school as obstacles. I didn't see. I saw you. Only you. How bad could that have been?

Seventeen years ago my choices were limited to the subjects I could teach and the proper role of a wife. None of the women who loved women lived openly together; public displays of affection, one hand lightly, humanly, touching another, were cause for arrest. In college, when we dared to go out to the bar, the streets were always thick with hatred. Gay-bashing and dyke-fucking were real sports. McCarthy was god; and Roy Cohn was a saint. This is what I am trying to explain to you. The only sex I ever had was quick; there was no time for lovemaking, foreplay or long champagne baths. You have no idea what it was like. For me. For them. For women like us who wanted to be together, there were no choices like you have today. It was not fair. I had to marry. After college, there was no genuine way to find each other.

Right after we were married and before the memories faded for good, I took the train into the city. It wasn't safe alone, but I had to go. Once inside the bar, a tattooed woman, dressed like a man, asked me to dance. As she circled me around the tiny dance floor, she drew me to her and our bodies met. From the moment I'd walked in, I was filled with desire and the agonizing fear that the red light would come on, signalling a raid. I knew if I was caught touching another woman, my name would be in all the papers. So after less than an hour, when the side of her hot face rested lightly next to mine, I stopped in the middle of the dance, left her warm cheek cold, and walked straight out the door. I don't know how I made it home and I never, ever went back.

Where I lived with David, I had no one to talk to. There were only young married pregnant women who weren't interested in careers of their own. But I found you on the tennis courts. I rescued both of us. I know I did. *That* is the history of women loving women. How we found each other, married or single, young or old, teacher or student. It didn't matter. There were no such things as boundaries because finding each other, anywhere, was a complete miracle. Instead of thanking me, you're telling me I hurt you. Why are you doing this?

I showed you the way; brought you into the life. I loved you, singled you out, and gave you my full attention. I don't understand what you want me to say. Would I do it all over again, if I had the chance? With you? Yes, of course. I loved you, love you, haven't stopped loving you all these years. You are saying we had different experiences. I don't understand. You never said no. Never said stop. Never said don't. I don't recognize you anymore.

Besides, I didn't see girls who took sports seriously. By the time I got them in junior high, all the girls hated Phys. Ed. You were different. You were an athlete, with proud parents. There was no sport you didn't excel in, although tennis was your sport. I couldn't let you go, or pretend I didn't notice. In college all the female coaches dreamed about students like you, serious female athletes. We saw ourselves as role models; we would fight for a place for young women in sports. Instead I was assigned over seventy students per class, rather than the usual thirty-five or forty kids. The other teachers made fun of me — *the anti-intellectual, the pig-head who stopped reading in college to play ball.* It was nothing like what we'd imagined. But the worst was the rumors. Everybody, from the janitors to the principal, thought any female coach was queer. Why else would she teach a "locker room" subject? I didn't have a chance. I couldn't so much as put an arm around a female student who fell on the basketball court, crying out in pain. I didn't dare touch any single student, rub shoulders, or even bear-hug with the winning team at the end of the game. And I had to teach in a pleated skirt, with shorts underneath and matching knee-socks.

When I graduated I chose to marry David because the rumors terrified me. I had convinced myself that he was a good man and that I wasn't queer. "Queers" were child molesters, dirty old men. Or big butches on motorcycles with red and green tattooes on their arms. I threw myself into my work, to finding any female students who took sports seriously. I didn't look or touch a single student until you. That's the truth. I no longer thought of myself as interested in women. I had distanced myself completely from any form of homosexuality. By then, just the thought of it, homoerotic love, made me sick. But seeing you on the court, I couldn't look away. From you. Or me. In my mind, I made a separate box for homosexuals, faggots and bull dykes. I put you and me in another corner of my brain, for protection. It was a huge risk to get involved. I could have lost my husband, my job and my license to teach — for good. Or been locked up in Women's Detention. How could I have possibly hurt you? The risk was all mine. I don't understand what you're saying. You were just a kid. I only wanted to show you the way.

When I finally told David that I was a lesbian, his first question was about you. After I answered, he sat down and cried, at the same kitchen table where the three of us had eaten our dinner. He said he felt so betrayed, and you're saying the same thing. I did love David, not exactly the way he loved me, but I was faithful to him the entire fifteen years of our marriage. I never looked at another man. He said that wasn't the point. The *point* was that I had lied to him. Then he drove away in the red Chevy wagon. That was the last time he ever spoke to me. Now you're saying that I lied to you too. But I gave you my best. I was completely faithful to both of you. This isn't fair. I am not a bad person. I am not a child molester. We had a relationship, you and me.

Don't you remember, when I kissed you, the first time? How good it felt to finally taste you in my mouth, me in yours? Our mouths together after months of waiting. We had made a wonderful dinner. Fried chicken wings and mashed potatoes — the small, red russet ones you always liked. You were leaving for vacation; I was scared. I knew I had to let you know what I was feeling and what I knew you were feeling for me. I got up to walk you to the door. In the hallway, away from David and the TV, I took your hand, then your arm. Reaching for your whole body, I pushed us both towards the wall. "Wait a minute," I whispered, trying to calm myself, "we're not going to see each other for a long time. Let's say good-bye the right way." Then you stopped, closed your eyes and waited. I couldn't stand the separation any longer. Pushing my legs up against your thighs, I pulled you to me before I lost my nerve. For the first time in over six years, I kissed a woman full-mouthed.

To be inside your mouth was wonderful. To taste you so close after waiting so long. In that single kiss, I forgot I was married, a teacher and thirteen years older than you. I remembered only my own hunger to be with a woman, hidden and suppressed for such a long time. I wanted the kiss to last through your vacation. So you'd come back wanting me as I wanted you. You were so full of passion; in that first kiss, I could feel how our bodies would come together. You're telling me now that you were scared. But you kissed me back. I remember my surprise — I thought I'd be the one to teach *you* how to kiss a woman. But you pushed hard your lips back on mine; you sucked my tongue as it came into your mouth. I don't believe you. You were hungry for me. I know you were. A kiss is a kiss. You kissed me back. That couldn't possibly have been the first time you ever kissed a woman. I want you to understand something; I didn't just love you, I adored you.

Yes. So I was in the closet. Until I was almost forty. That would make anybody crazy. I didn't even know I was in the closet. Or what the fucking closet was all about. There was no such thing as Gay Liberation. Just the thought of it makes me laugh. Why would I want to march down the street telling everybody I'm queer? Are you kidding? We had a good thing. Why are you doing this to me? Let me ask you something. If I hadn't been your teacher, and we'd met in the bar, would it all be okay? Then baby dyke and her seasoned lover would be sitting around, reminiscing about the early days. You'd be thanking me instead of cursing me like you're doing right this minute.

The way you're talking makes me wish I never had a dream to help young girls take themselves seriously as athletes. I could have gone into business; that was what I'd minored in. And then what? You would have grown up as I did. Feeling different, and loathing that very difference that's at the heart of who we are. If I'd left you as my student you would have been afraid and passed for straight like everybody else. All the while the pretense would have sucked the life out of you. Just as it did to me. No wonder I married David. Who the hell wants to be different?

I tried to make a way for you, and a path for both of us to follow. I couldn't do it alone. Now you want to hand me a therapy bill. You want me to pay for your rehabilitation, seventeen years later. Let me ask you something. You're queer, right? You've got a lover, a hot ticket, waiting for you as we speak. And you were queer back then. Right? So what's the problem? That's what I want to know. Because I didn't do anything to you. You were like that when I found you. That's the first truth that needs saying here: who we were when we found each other.

I never thought it would come to this. I always figured that you'd miss me and we'd end up together. But you never came back. And when you finally did, it wasn't to tell me how much you missed me. Loved me. Wanted me back. It wasn't at all the way I had imagined all these years. You came back to tell me that I hurt you; that it was too much, too soon; that I should've been a good friend rather than your lover. Well, you have your memories, and I've got mine. I can't believe that's all we have left — two different sets of memories, miles apart. The way you're talking, you'd think we weren't even speaking about the same event. That we'd never been lovers. Never been in love. Planned a whole future together. Laughed. Cried in each other's arms. You're talking as though you want to arrest me, after all these years. But what makes your version any truer than mine? Because you're not the only one who knows what happened back then. I know what happened. And I know who we were for each other; what we did, together. I haven't forgotten, not in seventeen years. Even if you have.

O

Zmira

Dinners on Friday evening are Zmira's favorite; it's the only time of the week the table is noisy. When Poppa asks Zmira what she learned in Hebrew school she sings a new Hebrew song. Afterward, Zmira is permitted to tell about public school and the fifth grade. On *Shabes* she has everyone's attention until dessert. All week Zmira plans what she will say to her poppa's *Shabes* guests.

In between bites of roast chicken and sips of grape juice Zmira announces that the fifth grade had tryouts for the school play. Zmira sees her mother nodding so she wipes her napkin over the juice spots decorating the space above her lips and below her nose and continues her story without stopping.

She had tried out for the play. Miss Alexander said if she wanted a big part to open her mouth very wide and let the words scream out. Zmira had been practicing opening her mouth very wide, letting all the words scream out. While she talks, Zmira sees her poppa looking at her mother. But her mother doesn't look up from her plate. Poppa's guests are eating very fast; Zmira knows they like her mother's cooking, but they are eating too fast to taste the special food. She hopes that no one will choke on her mother's roast chicken and brown potatoes.

Zmira watches everyone watching Poppa. She thinks they are waiting to see what he will say to ten-year-old Zmira about her school play. Zmira remembers that Poppa always tells his guests to leave the problems of the outside world outside the weekly festival. Zmira wants to tell everyone that the name of the play is *Tom Sawyer* with songs and dances written by the music and drama teachers. But no one is talking to Zmira; not even *Bobe* and *Zayde*. All the guests are watching Poppa who is chewing very fast the last piece of roast chicken on his plate.

Poppa is ready for dessert; he wants to say grace after the meal and bid his guests good-bye. Zmira thinks she said something wrong because her favorite meal is over early. She reminds herself that the school play is just like *Purim* when she dresses up as Queen Esther and pretends to rescue all the Jewish people from the wicked Haman. No one is talking to Zmira. When she clears the table, Zmira doesn't feel the *Shabes* warmth surrounding her. The candles still burn but their light isn't the usual yellow brightness Zmira dreams about all week.

Before Zmira goes to bed Poppa asks his daughter if she received a part in the school play. He wants to know when the play is scheduled for production. Zmira tells her poppa, Nathan, that everyone in the two fifth grades has a part, but no one will know until Monday exactly what character they will be. The play will be performed in the middle of December, before Christmas vacation. Four weeks seems like a long time to wait. When Nathan finishes his questions he walks out of the room without saying good night to his *Shabes* princess. Esther reminds Zmira to wear her green dress, Nathan's favorite, tomorrow. Alone in her room, Zmira wonders what happened at the *Shabes* table? *Bobe* didn't drink all her wine and *Zayde's* eyes didn't shine when he kissed Zmira good-bye.

Shabes is half over; but Nathan hasn't told a *Shabes* story. He makes them up each week for Zmira. She likes the one about the old man who went one *Shabes* to heaven and one *Shabes* to hell, to see where the festival celebration is best. In hell everyone wears chains on their arms. No one eats roast chicken; they only stare at the sweet food, starving. In heaven, people wear chains too. Zmira was given a week to find out how the people in heaven are able to eat. All week she couldn't look at her poppa; no one she asked knew the answer. In Hebrew school they told her to ask Nathan Rabinowitz, her poppa; he knew all the answers.

The next week Nathan told the entire *Shabes* table that the people in heaven feed each other. That's why no one is hungry. He told his guests that the Jews had done this for over four thousand years and must continue to do so or the Messiah will not come.

Later Zmira asked her poppa, "When will the Messiah come?" Poppa said the Messiah will come dressed as a beggar, hungry, when we least expect the Holy One. Zmira thinks that the Messiah is just like a part in the school play, when all the real people dress up and pretend to be someone else.

Zmira is Hebrew for melody. Everyone at *shul* calls her Nathan's little melody. Poppa asks Zmira to sing the festival melodies when he returns from *davening*. Zmira doesn't mind singing for Esther or Nathan, but Poppa always brings home a few old *tzadikim* from *shul*. Nathan calls them the wise ones. Zmira thinks they must be almost a hundred; at least seven long-bearded faces come to the house every Saturday afternoon. They bless the wine, break the *challah* and walk right into Nathan's study, calling for the melody to follow. Zmira is sure that none of the *tzadikim* listen when she sings. How could they? As soon as she begins, their eyes close; Nathan's eyes close first. After twenty minutes, Zmira tiptoes out, running through the house looking for her mother who gives her hot tea with honey and a *Shabes* cookie, cut in a half moon, frosted white and blue in honor of the State of Israel. They sit together and Zmira asks Esther to explain her poppa to her one more time.

"He works hard," her mother nods but doesn't smile whenever she talks to Zmira about Nathan. "He works with numbers — making other men's accounts work out. The *shul* would be lost without Nathan Rabinowitz; he manages all the numbers. And he *davens* three times a day, every day. He leaves early in the morning, stopping for a few minutes with his God before work, in the middle of the afternoon and again before he leaves his office for home. Zmira, Poppa is often the tenth man in the *minyan;* he's a good man."

Zmira used to pretend she was the tenth man in the *minyan* until Nathan found out and told her never to do that again. The *minyan,* he said, belongs to the men, especially the *tzadikim,* not to little girls or women.

Esther said that Nathan was his father's only son. There were three daughters. He was their first little *tzadik.* His father waited for the day when Zmira's poppa would be a *Bar Mitzvah,* a man. Zmira's head is hurting. A man at thirteen, then her poppa went to work and learned *Torah* better than his own father. He is the pride of the *shul.* Esther explains that because Zmira is an only child, she must be son and daughter to her poppa. Zmira's head is heavy; she feels herself slipping off the chair and onto the rug. Esther catches her. She holds Zmira's head in her lap. Zmira licks the icing off her cookie and pretends she is kissing the State of Israel at the same time. When she sings today, the old men close their eyes, but Nathan says they listen, hearing even the pauses between each line.

The old men scratch their beards, adjust their *yarmulkes* on the back of their heads, and say good-bye to Nathan. The rest of the day, like every *Shabes* afternoon, is spent with Nathan, dressed in his black suit and thin black tie holding his neck straight, reading the weekly *Torah* portion in his study. Esther rests on the couch, and Zmira plays alone on the rug in front of the couch. Nathan forbids his family to do any everyday activities during the weekly festival. He tells Esther and Zmira that all the Rabinowitzes follow the tradition of the People Israel. Zmira knows that the last *Shabes* meal will be in silence. She will have to wait an entire week before her family and her Poppa's guests sit together again at the noisy festival table.

Sunday is a work day even though the schools are closed. Nathan leaves the house early to pray and to work on his accounts. He covers his head with a small brown hat when he walks in the street, refusing to take his uncovered head out into the city. Zmira thinks he looks better in his brown felt hat than in his *yarmulke*. She likes the way this bulky man looks as he walks down the street: tall and big, the brown hat makes her poppa stick out on street corners when people crowd together, waiting to cross to the other side.

On Monday Zmira finds her name close to the top of the auditions list. She is assigned the part of a grandmother, a *bobe*. She wants to ask her own *bobe* if she can wear her shawl, the old, dirty-colored one that's supposed to be white. Someone in the family made the shawl for Esther's mother, no one remembers who. "A friend for my wedding," that's what *Bobe* says. Whoever made the shawl had strong hands; the stitches are small, tied tightly in and out of each other, like kids in a circle holding hands so hard that there isn't a real beginning or end. On *Shabes,* when she has to be quiet, Zmira stares at the woven knots. Closing her eyes, she imagines the hands of *Bobe's* friend Rivka, big and strong, working an entire afternoon without stopping, knitting the thick wool into the soft beautiful shawl for *Bobe*. Miss Alexander tells Zmira that the shawl would be a fine addition to her costume.

In preparation for the school play, classes finish each day at two, and an hour is spent in rehearsal. Twenty-five children make up the chorus. They have eight songs to learn, each leading role will have a solo to sing. Zmira grins like *Zayde* does on Friday nights. No one had told her she would be singing for the fifth grade school play. In the middle of her excitement Zmira remembers that Poppa has forgotten to ask her the name of her school play.

During the week Nathan refuses to go over Zmira's lines with her. She wants to practice together, the same way he always practices the Hebrew blessings with her before each holiday. Zmira's mother says that Poppa is busy all day. He comes home tired and needs to be alone with God. So they must be quiet when they rehearse Zmira's lines in the living room, right next to Poppa's study. After the first two-and-a-half weeks of practice Nathan tells Zmira and Esther that Mr. Sawyer is disturbing his concentration and must remain at school; he's not to come home with Zmira again.

On Thursday Poppa asks Zmira if she knows any other stories besides her Mr. Sawyer story. Zmira doesn't recognize Nathan; his whole face is one giant frown. She thinks he could frighten even the numbers on the page in front of him while he works on his accounts. Poppa says that Esther has too many holidays to prepare for and where is Zmira's head that she needs calling more than once to help her mother? He tells Zmira that the Ten Commandments leave no question: "Honor thy Father and thy Mother." Zmira helps Esther make the *challah* this week; she learns to braid the sticky round piles into the thick *Shabes* loaves that she loves.

This *Shabes* the house is especially noisy. The guests tease Zmira, asking her how she feels to be a *bobe* and to be so young and so old at the same time. Just as Zmira giggles and starts to talk like the *bobe* in *Tom Sawyer* Nathan calls for dessert, and for Zmira to clear the table. Then he ends Zmira's favorite meal with grace and good-bye to his guests. Zmira looks around the table; maybe God forgot to bless them tonight.

In the middle of the week Zmira tells her mother that the school play is scheduled for December fifteenth, right after *Chanukah*. Right away we'll have another celebration, a *simcha*. Zmira wants to invite all her poppa's *Shabes* guests to her very own *simcha*. *Tom Sawyer* is a good story, Zmira explains. Miss

Alexander says it's an all-American classic. Her poppa will want to sit in the front row like he does at *shul*. Will all the *Shabes* guests want to sit in the front row? At practice, which is more fun than Hebrew school, Miss Alexander told the class that there will be a cast party.

Zmira asks herself, what's happening to her poppa, her *Shabes* prince? He makes all the festivals brighter; it's Poppa's face that always lifts high above the festival lights. He finds Zmira's eyes across the table. In between the flickering light they wink at each other, prince and princess. But now, she can not find his eyes. They don't reach out for her above the flames. She can't remember when poppa last told a *Shabes* story. The stories are for her, his melody; all the guests know that. Zmira watches Nathan pull on his beard. His fingers tug at the long strands of grey hair. On the way home from *shul* Nathan forgets to remove his *yarmulke* and Zmira laughs when her poppa walks into the house, stopping to kiss the *mezuzah*. Zmira thinks her poppa has taken his whole life growing tall enough to kiss the *mezuzah* on the front door. She looks for a *mezuzah* on the public school doors, in her classroom and on the double doors to the auditorium.

When Zmira tells her poppa that the play is in two weeks, Nathan reminds his daughter that the first night of *Chanukah* is just ten days away. Then Zmira giggles and says she has two holidays this year; she doesn't know which one is better. Esther spills soup on her way to the table; Zmira wants to know if the whole family will sit in the front row. Nathan says his soup is too hot. He asks Zmira to learn the *Chanukah* blessings by heart this year. Then he says good night. Zmira sees that her mother has made her poppa's favorite meal, stuffed cabbage — and it's not even a holiday.

Miss Alexander wants to know how many extra free tickets Zmira will need. Each student with a big part may have more than two tickets. Zmira says she will have at least two more — for *Bobe* and *Zayde*. The week before the play, Zmira can't sit still at her desk. Miss Alexander wants to know if she's sick. Zmira thinks her body isn't big enough for all the fun she's having with her fifth grade class. She wants to give everyone in the play a big hug, but she doesn't know who to hug first.

At home she doesn't feel like hugging anybody, especially her poppa. The house feels almost dead, nobody laughs and giggles like in the fifth grade. Zmira decides that the fifth grade is the best grade; she wants to be a fifth grader for the rest of her life. All the kids put their milk money in a box, to buy Miss Alexander a bouquet of flowers for a surprise. Zmira tells her poppa it's just like Hebrew school when the light blue can with the State of Israel painted on both sides is passed around and everyone gives *tzedakah* to plant almond trees in the holy land. The surprise is red carnations. Zmira wants to know why her poppa doesn't ever surprise Esther or Zmira with red carnations, or even a bouquet of flowers.

This week *Shabes* rushes in. As soon as the guests seat themselves in their usual places, and before all the blessings are finished, Zmira takes over the table. She invites everyone to see *Tom Sawyer,* an all-American classic. The guests look at Nathan, waiting for him to bless the *challah.* Zmira explains there are twenty seats on the right side, front row, of the auditorium. She can have as many seats as she needs in that row for the first night of the play. When Miss Alexander approved the seating she asked Zmira if the whole synagogue was coming. Zmira thinks that's a great idea so all the *Shabes* guests are invited to the play. Zmira requested the front row because of her poppa; he always sits in the front row, on the right hand side of the *shul.* Nathan blesses the *challah* and passes the bread around for everyone to break off a piece. He explains to his guests that they are not expected to attend his daughter's play. He knows they have better things to do than watch a bunch of fifth graders run around in all directions on a stage, making too much noise. He adds that both he and his wife Esther plan not to attend the performance.

He will no doubt be needed at the *shul; Chanukah* always messes up the accounts considerably.

While she eats, Zmira Rabinowitz listens to her poppa laughing with his guests. Why doesn't he want to see her all dressed up like *Bobe*? She closes her eyes when Nathan says grace and pictures herself on stage with *Bobe's* dirty-colored shawl, staring out at the empty first row on the right hand side of the auditorium. She keeps her eyes closed long enough for the stage to become the *bima* at the front of the *shul* where the Rebbe stands. From the center of the *bima* Zmira sees her poppa sitting in the front row, *davening*. He turns the pages of his *siddur* without looking up at Zmira, who is singing a solo on the *bima*.

Zmira cannot imagine singing a solo on the stage. She closes her eyes until the picture of herself standing alone disappears.

O

Her Job

She is going to try now for the first time to remember everything but especially how she is sitting downstairs listening to the whole thing happen. With her mother and her sister she sits downstairs in the living room waiting. She cannot remember where her sister sits. Maybe she sits alone on the couch all alone. Their mother sits on a twin armchair. She sits on the other twin armchair. Her father is upstairs with her other sister who is upstairs with her father. What do they do waiting until it's over in the living room? They are waiting. They do not talk except when she looks at her mother and her mother says it hurts him much more than it will ever hurt her. They do not talk they wait for it to be over. All the sounds all the sounds of the belt. The shiny black belt her father wears when he dresses to go out with her mother. The shiny black belt with the small gold buckle that looks like a small fork for spooning out grapefruit that her father wears when he dresses to go out with her mother. She tries to imagine what she cannot see. She knows the door is closed the door to the room where her father and her sister are is closed. How does she know the door where her father and her sister are is closed. She knows (she knows) the door is closed. She does not even imagine the door closed. The door is closed. There is no door in the living room where she sits with her mother and her sister waiting. The living room is a completely open room. There are only doorways. She thinks they are in the guest room with red wallpaper and white dots at the top of the stairs. She tries to imagine what she cannot see behind the closed door. She imagines they are sitting somewhere in the guest room. There is only one chair a rocking chair that her mother painted red to match the red and white wallpaper. There are no cushions on the rocking chair it is not a comfortable chair. The rocking chair came with the big white house. It is made of wood from the lumber yard of the people who lived here first. The red rocker moves. She wonders if it is moving now back and forth. When she sits in it by herself holding onto the wooden arms she rocks herself gently back and forth. She pushes her back all the way into the back of the chair. She imagines her father pushing his back all the way into the chair. With her sister on his lap the red rocker moves rocking back and forth. They don't talk much her mother her sister and her. They are waiting they are waiting for it to be over. She does not know how long they are waiting. She knows she is not allowed to move. She knows she is not allowed to move just like she knows the door upstairs is closed. She doesn't think she could move even if she did move she must sit and listen. This is her job. She is trying to remember she is trying to remember if there really are any sounds or if she only imagines them. This is her job. There are things she wants to know if her sister has her panties on the ones with the white lace around the edges that their mother bought on sale at Woolworth's Department Store the day before Halloween. There are things she wants to know if her sister doesn't have her Halloween panties on who pulled the panties down because they have elastic and fit tight around the waist. If the panties are off are they lying around her ankles or are they curled up in a ball on the red carpet lying next to the moving rocking chair. There are things she wants to know does her sister still have her good pumps on that she came home from the high school in or did they slip off her feet one at a time. Does her sister push up her brown plaid skirt all the way above her waistline or does she unzip the zipper letting the skirt fall straight down around her ankles. Does she step out of the loop the skirt made in a pile on the carpet and then bend down to fold the skirt up neatly. There are things she wants to know like what is it like to be upstairs in the guest room with their father alone with the door closed with her sister's plain skirt probably pushed up around her waist and her panties pulled down around her ankles. How exactly is her sister sitting on her father's lap. She must be bent over in a position that's different from when she sits in her father's lap waiting for a hug. Where is her sister's face her face must be pointing down to the red carpet with her whole head sticking out through the arms of the rocking chair that is made of wood from the lumberyard of the people who lived in the big white house first. What about her sister's eyes. Are they looking are they staring straight ahead at the red and white wallpaper. What are they seeing her sister's two brown eyes. Or are they closed. Her own eyes are staring into the living room staring into the living room that is a completely open room waiting. Waiting for it to be over. There are things she wants to know does her sister have any clothes on is her sister naked if her sister is naked is her father naked too. She knows that it is her sister who does not have any clothes on she does not know how she knows this she knows her father has his clothes on. The real problem is that she cannot hear if there are any sounds or if she only imagines all the sounds she does not hear any sounds. She closes her eyes she tries to imagine silent sounds. Silence without sounds coming from the guest room upstairs with the door closed and her sister's panties pulled down. And then she sees her sister's legs sticking out the other end of the rocker opposite from where her sister's head is sticking out. She has forgotten about her sister's legs. Her own legs are bent at the knee and held tight together but she knows her sister's legs are not bent at the knee. That would be impossible. She knows they are sticking straight out the other side of the rocker like a piece of lumber from the lumberyard. When she knows her sister is spread out like a piece of lumber she is afraid her sister will hurt her head on the arm of the rocking chair. She does not want her sister to hit her head because then her sister's neck will break and she will never be able to sit up straight again. She doesn't want her sister's neck to break. To break means there is a noise crack snap she doesn't want her sister's neck to break. She is listening for all the sounds she doesn't hear from the guest room where the door is closed. There are things she wants to know what happened to the sound. The sound. Where is the sound. They are waiting downstairs in the living room for it to be over. Her mother her sister and her. They are waiting for the sounds they do not hear to stop. There is a sound she hears the sound of a shiny black belt. The sound of the belt is the only sound she hears. She hears the black belt snap back and forth once in the air and once where her sister's panties are either on or off. The only sound she hears is the sound of a snapping black belt. There are other things she wants to know what happened to the sound the sound of her sister with her father alone in the guest room in the red and white rocking chair where the door is closed. The door is closed. They are waiting waiting without making a sound her mother her sister and her.

There are things she wants to know is it real if it only happened once. Is once enough to count. There is no one to ask she wants to ask her sister the one it happened to. There are things she wants to know. What happened to the sound. The sound of her sister with her father in the guest room and the sound of waiting. Waiting in the living room for it to be over.

O

The State of Extreme Agitation

Long ago there lived an extremely agitated student of the *Talmud* whose name was Aryeh Simcha Chernokovich. The source of his agitation, however, was unknown, even to himself. The village had its speculators and at least once a week Shlomo the dairy man and Yitzhak the butcher could be heard in the alley behind the dirt road that led to the old cemetery, exchanging competing speculations.

"It's the boy's brilliance," Shlomo cried, "what's driving him crazy. After all, he's the smartest in his class; there's no one smarter than he in the entire village, including our very own Rebbe!"

Yitzhak shook his head, spitting once to the right and once to the left. "Don't speak such blasphemy in this town. The boy needs a wife, that's all."

But Shlomo persisted, for he had experienced personally the youth's erudition. Once, when the Rebbe took sick, leaving the village without an advisor, the unseasoned scholar stepped forward offering to solve whatever controversies arose during the Rebbe's untimely illness.

The people froze in their boots at the insolent youth's offer. No one could replace their Rebbe. Now, it just so happened that the village was in the midst of a huge argument with Shlomo the dairy man and in need of immediate assistance.

The women cried out that they could no longer afford to feed their families if Shlomo continued to raise the price of his milk.

Quickly, the wise young pupil seized the moment, pausing only to adjust his *yarmulke*. He spoke as fast as he could. "As to the question of the milk…"

Shlomo watched as the words flew out of the pupil's mouth, leapt off his moving lips and landed directly inside the angry ears of the wild crowd. In an instant the entire village erupted in silence. For they had experienced firsthand the true brilliance of the one who stood before them.

Within three days, the prices of milk dropped dramatically and Shlomo's business continued to prosper. A week later, the dairy man was seen feeding six new cows, while news of Ari's wisdom travelled far and wide.

Soon after the crisis in milk, his own agitation had begun to make the quick-tongued scholar quite irritable. Even his nights were full of fitful sleep. It got so bad that Ari decided to do something about the situation; he decided to become a Doctor of Acute Observation, and thus observe himself. In doing so, he discovered there were three precise moments when the agitation increased and became impossible to suppress.

The first happened whenever he studied with Barach, who was known to be his only rival and with whom he had conferred about the problem of the milk. Whenever he sat with Barach for more than an hour, he would become so deeply engrossed in the text that their collective brilliance took hold of their bodies and more often than not, in the midst of a fine point in their discourse of the *midrash* — not obvious to any of the other students — the two men would clasp hands, staring fiercely into the other's eyes.

Ari had always assumed that when their hands met they were meeting in celebration of the *Talmud.* But as a Doctor of Acute Observation, he had to admit that he never wanted to remove his hand from Barach's after the moment of radiant exclamation ceased to burn between them. Reluctantly though, Ari would remove his hand. Then the agitation would begin in earnest.

The second time he observed himself in agitation was just before the evening prayers, especially before the Sabbath, when he and Barach *davened* together; their bodies bowed and swayed with the fervor of their hearts. If he even glanced at his dazzling rival, his entire body broke out in a cold sweat, beginning with his palms then spreading rapidly to the skin beneath his *tzizis.*

The third occasion of his agitation occurred whenever he was about to leave the *Yeshiva.* Ari boarded at the widow Gulden's house, but Barach slept at the old dormitory beyond the school. In leaving for the night, he had to leave Barach. And as a Doctor of Acute Observation, he observed that it was his very own leaving that left him in total agitation.

Aryeh Simcha Chernokovich knew enough not to tell a living soul about his acute observations, not even Barach. But he knew he had to discuss his situation with someone. For what he had come to realize was that he loved Barach not like a brother but as a Sabbath Bride, and that his agitation would fail to cease unless his love was consummated.

Chernokovich knew his feelings were unacceptable. Yet in all his studies, he had found no rational explanation for the rejection of his love. So he determined to speak with the great Reb Skolnik, who lived hundreds of miles away.

He packed his bags and went at once; on foot by day, at night sleeping in any doorway he could find, which was not hard because his reputation for brilliance preceded him. Wherever he went the villagers begged for the chance to house the luminous scholar. To shelter the head that protected such genius, huge feather pillows were piled high around his bed. At night, terrified his dreams would betray him, Chernokovich remained awake, singing *Adon Olam,* praising God backwards and forwards, lest anyone become privy to his desire for Barach.

Finally, after weeks of walking and worrying, Chernokovich arrived on the doorstep of Reb Skolnik's house and knocked softly. But even before he had finished, the door opened. The ·Rebbe ushered him in.

"You're late. I've been waiting for you since yesterday. What took you so long?"

"Reb Skolnik, I must ask you a most difficult question. A question I can ask no one but yourself."

"First, we must have some tea. I want also to show you my new samovar, sent to the Rebbetzin and myself from a childless couple who just had their first son. Then we'll eat a little; there's no hurry. Later, you'll ask that question of yours. We shall see what the answer is together, for my intellect is no greater than your own."

"But Reb Skolnik, this is not such a question I can answer myself. I've tried, believe me."

"Have some tea." The Rebbe moved slowly, while the young scholar could barely contain himself. So as not to appear insolent, he tried to admire Reb Skolnik's new samovar. He knew that when the Rebbe was ready to talk they would talk, and not a moment sooner.

"A sugar cube?" Reb Skolnik sat down. Together the men silently gazed upon the shining new samovar. "Your journey here was without mishap, I presume?" The Rebbe paced himself, not wanting to jump in before assessing the mental aptitude of the one who sought him out. After all, most who sought the

Rebbe's wisdom did so in far more indirect ways, not daring to come to his doorstep uninvited.

Chernokovich knew the Rebbe was infamous for drinking tea with his guests for hours before the official meeting began, yet he could wait no longer. So full of longing were his days that he determined to beg the Rebbe to stall no more. Instead, he heard himself ask for a second cup of tea.

"But of course. And take some jam with your bread. Perhaps you want to rest before we begin?" The Rebbe was pleased; he had begun to form a sense of the seeker who sat before him. This was no ordinary *shealah ketanah,* no easy question that lay beneath the surface.

"Reb Skolnik, forgive my impudence, but I must speak." Chernokovich was shocked; he had been unable to hold himself back. Surely his manner betrayed him. Any moment he would be sent away without hesitation.

But the wise teacher only smiled. What question could so consume such a young mind as to escape uncontrolled from the youthful scholar's lips? A similar passion he had not witnessed since his own fervor burst forth years earlier in *Yeshiva.* He recalled the smug faces of his disciples, so lacking in humility he feared their cunning would cause the Jewish people immense sorrow.

"I see your journey has exhausted you. Let us say the evening prayers. In the morning you shall ask your question." So grateful was Chernokovich not to have been sent out, back into the streets because of his rudeness, that he accepted without challenge the Rebbe's suggestion of sleep. In fact, he welcomed the opportunity to prepare in earnest the precise wording of his question — now that he knew he would actually have a chance to speak.

After *davening ma'ariv,* Chernokovich was shown a sofa in the hallway behind the Rebbetzin's kitchen where, as soon as his head reached the first pillow, he fell instantly and deeply asleep for the first time in months. He woke rested the next morning only to be seized with a huge panic because he had not spent the night adequately preparing his question.

But when he followed Reb Skolnik back into the study where they sat only yesterday drinking tea from the shining samovar, Chernokovich saw that he was prepared in spite of himself. In fact, he had been preparing his entire life for just this moment. He had arrived at that place in his studies that few among them ever reach.

To those who read the words of the *Torah,* not only with their minds, but with their hearts and souls bound up together in the holy tongue, there comes a moment when either wholeness of mind and body occur or a crisis of faith erupts instead. Rarely do those who experience crisis over wholeness live to tell the next generation. To date, Chernokovich had heard only of the ones reaching wholeness. The others disappeared; the memory of their names went with them into the faithless wilderness.

But Chernokovich was determined that his crisis of faith — as he had just this second come to understand it — would not outlive him. No, wholeness would be his. And with a sudden surge of his head, he seized the Rebbe's attention, prepared to ask his question.

The Rebbe, attentive to every nuance occurring in his presence, knew that the young pupil had arrived early in his lifetime at the famed moment. In fact, the previous evening, he blessed its coming before kissing the Rebbetzin goodnight.

"Well, let us hear the question."

Looking at the wall beyond the great teacher and gripping both arms of his chair, Chernokovich felt the agitation overcome him. Nonetheless he plunged into his question. "Reb Skolnik, can you tell me, why is it forbidden for a man to love another man?"

The Rebbe, startled but not shocked, said, "Why, because it is against all of nature."

"Just whose nature is it against?"

"Yours and mine."

"But Reb Skolnik, of your nature it may be against, but of mine, I'm not so sure. Who is to say what becomes one man's nature must then become another's?" Chernokovich could not believe his own words, let alone that he sat now in front of the great Reb Skolnik, a true *tzadik godol*, daring to disagree.

The Rebbe, a wise and patient man, a brilliant thinker in his own right, saw in an instant the keen intelligence of the one who sat before him. He saw too that this was no ordinary crisis of faith. Sitting before him was truly a man in search of God.

He thought before he spoke. "When Noah filled his ark, two-by-two all the animals of the land took shelter; two-by-two, male and female together, they sought refuge. So it is with man."

"But Rebbe, my refuge is as David's was in Jonathan, and my shelter is as theirs." Chernokovich had poured over and over the Bible, that section in the Book of Samuel, where David proclaimed his love for Jonathan. Nowhere was their specific love condemned.

Rather, Chernokovich had come to see it was the unspecific and wanton lust of a man for his brother that was actually *treyf*. And this he knew the Rebbe knew too. Lust itself was the forbidden fruit, for it made an object out of love.

Reb Skolnik had met his match; and the consequence of such a perfect symmetry was that the *Talmud* lay open before them, equal in interpretation. "The problem is not David and Jonathan, as you well have reminded us, but rather the problem is with their descendants. If all of us loved as they, no one would live to usher in the Messiah; the earth would lie barren, the fields fallow, and the *Torah* would remain unopened."

The room grew still upon the completion of the Rebbe's words. So strong was the presence of silence between them, it was as though the scholars were no longer alone. Chernokovich wondered if the souls of Jonathan and David bound together for all eternity had not entered Reb Skolnik's study. In the depth of the stillness Chernokovich sought refuge from the Rebbe's last point. For it was the place in his own mind that he most feared to look. What the Rebbe had suggested was that David's love for Jonathan, however good and pure it was, did not secure the future of their people.

In the midst of their silence Chernokovich's passion grew larger than his fear of the Rebbe's words. In his fervor he saw that the sages knew all too well how strong a man's love for his brother could be. And that this love was as natural as another man's love for his wife. So it had to be forbidden.

His heart ached but Chernokovich plunged himself deeper into the abyss. Why could not the two coexist, since all of Judaism was built around dualities — light and darkness, the Sabbath and the six secular days of the week, Israel and the rest of the world? So too, a man's love for his wife could live in harmony with another man's love for his brother.

To Chernokovich, the problem seemed to be that the sages had given far too much attention to this other form of loving and so it had to be forbidden. If the love of David and Jonathan had been allowed to flourish, each man would be free to follow his own nature. And the People Israel would continue to flourish, because it is upon dualities that the world depends for balance.

What the sages had done in their fear of difference was to impose a singular form which all love had to reflect. And in that one gesture they hoped to secure the People Israel for the coming of the Messiah. Yet, in their fear, they only secured the eternal imbalance of the world.

So long had the room been filled with the thick air of Chernokovich's pensive thoughts that he feared the Rebbe's patience had left him. After all, the two men had been sitting for hours. In fact they had missed *davening minchah,* so deep were they tied to their discourse.

Finally, Chernokovich spoke what he knew to be his last words before the great teacher. "Reb Skolnik, I see that my quarrel is not with God but with man, because I too am created in God's image. My heart is full with a sorrow which no woman can fill. I shall live the rest of my days alone before I shall live with a wife without love. Is there anything else you can tell me?"

The Rebbe foresaw the young man's arrival and now felt his departure. He knew there was yet a single reason left for the separation of the same sexes. And although it was not written anywhere in the text, everywhere it was hinted at. In keeping with the tradition, the Rebbe had always refrained from speaking aloud this truth. Now it was he who prepared himself to speak.

He looked pained, then disturbed, then utterly perturbed. Finally, after several moments of prolonged silence, he shook his head sadly, leaned forward and whispered, "But what would the *goyim* think?"

Chernokovich was stunned. He had to admit that he was not prepared for a revelation such as this. He stared at the Rebbe, momentarily speechless, for he realized that the gates of *Yerushalayim* had just opened before him. And all the words of the *Torah* lay bare.

The meaning of the Rebbe's disclosure bore down upon the shoulders of Chernokovich. The Rebbe had stated a *midrash* far more complex than he had yet to confront, causing the scholar severe discomfort. *With whom could he speak such a truth?* The Rebbe sat back in his chair, exhausted from the weight of his own knowledge. As he stared into the eyes of the youthful one who sat before him, the *Torah* slowly passed from one generation to the next.

O Glossary

Adon Olam: (Hebrew) Song/prayer in praise of God, traditionally sung at the end of the Shabbat service.

aliyah: (Hebrew) When a member of the congregation is called to recite a blessing in honor of the *Torah.* The term is also used to refer to Jews who move permanently to Israel.

Barach: (Yiddish and Hebrew) A man's name, originating from the Hebrew word meaning blessing.

Bat Mitzvah: (Yiddish and Hebrew) Ceremony for girls when they reach the age of twelve or thirteen, welcoming them into the Jewish community as adults. Similar to the *Bar Mitzvah* for boys, who are welcomed at the age of thirteen.

bima: (Hebrew) A raised platform in the sanctuary of the synagogue where the Rabbi and cantor stand. The religious service is led from the *bima,* and the ark that holds the *Torah* is placed here.

Bube: (Yiddish) Grandmother.

brokhe: (Yiddish and Hebrew) A blessing.

challah: (Yiddish and Hebrew) Braided egg-bread. It is braided to symbolize the intertwining of our lives with that of God's. It is eaten on *Shabbat* and other holidays, except Passover, where bread is not eaten.

Chanukah: (Hebrew) Festival of Lights. During a period of unrest, the Temple at Jerusalem was destroyed. Only one day's supply of oil remained for the eternal lamp. The holiday celebrates the miracle of this oil lasting for eight days, keeping the sacred lamp alight, and giving a runner enough time to find more fuel. The festival honors the victory of the Jewish Maccabbees, who saved the Jews from destruction and from forced conversion by the Assyrians in 168 B.C.

chupah: (Yiddish and Hebrew) A sacred canopy that the bride and groom stand under during the marriage ceremony.

davens, davening: (Yiddish and Hebrew) Praying; the physical act of praying.

glatt kosher: (Yiddish and Hebrew) Food that meets the religious and dietary laws of orthodox Judaism as delineated in the *Torah,* such as the separation of milk and meat and the exclusion of forbidden foods, such as shellfish, from the diet.

goyim: (Yiddish and Hebrew) All non-Jews, gentiles.

goyishe: (Yiddish) Adjective. All things not Jewish.

Juden: (German) Jew

Kaddish: (Hebrew) The Jewish prayer for the dead.

kashrut: (Yiddish and Hebrew) The laws referring to ritually clean and permitted food, kosher food.

kosher: Food that meets the laws of the *kashrut,* and has been properly prepared according to these laws.

ma'ariv: (Hebrew) Evening prayers.

mezuzah: (Yiddish and Hebrew) A beautiful, religious ceremonial object containing the Ten Commandments. Jews place the *mezuzahs* on the door posts of their houses to establish that the home is a Jewish home, as they are commanded to do in the *Torah.*

midrash: (Yiddish and Hebrew) Commentary on the weekly *Torah* portion.

minchah: (Hebrew) Afternoon prayers.

minyan: (Yiddish and Hebrew) The ten men necessary, according to orthodox Judaism, before religious services can begin: women are counted in the *minyan* in all other branches of Judaism.

Purim: (Yiddish and Hebrew) The Feasts of Lots. The holiday celebrating the destruction of Haman, who wanted to destroy all the Jews in Persia, and honoring Queen Esther, who is responsible for saving her people.

Rabbi: (Hebrew) Jewish spiritual, religious leader and scholar.

Ramah: (Hebrew) A name used by the Conservative (as opposed to Reform or Orthodox) Jewish movement to refer to summer camps for Jewish children to learn about Jewish culture and religion.

Rebbe: (Yiddish) see Rabbi.

Rebbetzin: (Hebrew and Yiddish) Wife of the Rabbi.

Rosh Hashanah: (Hebrew) Literal meaning: Head of the New Year: Holiday that celebrates the Jewish New Year based on the lunar calendar.

shochet: (Yiddish) Kosher butcher.

shul: (Yiddish) Synagogue.

seder: (Hebrew) Literally meaning 'order', as in the correct placement of things. The name for the meal eaten the first two nights of Passover, which includes the telling of the History of the Jews from slavery to freedom. The meal includes special food, song and prayer.

Shabbat: (Hebrew) Weekly Jewish festival beginning at sundown on Friday and ending at sundown on Saturday, celebrating the completion of creation. *Shabbat* is the Sabbath, a day of prayer and rest.

Shabes: (Yiddish) see Shabbat.

shealah ketanah: (Yiddish and Hebrew) A little. A small question, not of huge significance.

shiksa: (Yiddish) A non-Jewish woman.

shiva· (Hebrew) Seven-day mourning period for Jews.

shlepping: (Yiddish) A form of walking which is really dragging or 'pulling' the feet along slowly.

Shlomo: (Yiddish and Hebrew) A man's name from the Hebrew word *shalom* or peace.

siddur: (Yiddish and Hebrew) Prayer book.

simcha: (Yiddish) A joyous occasion.

Talmud: (Yiddish and Hebrew) Sixty-three books containing interpretations and discussions of the *Torah* by Rabbis and scholars; consisting of the *Mishnah* (codified oral law) and the *Gemorah* (the written law).

Torah: (Yiddish and Hebrew) The Five Books Of Moses, the "Old" Testament: Genesis, Exodus, Leviticus, Numbers, and Deuteronomy: Jewish law.

treyf: (Yiddish and Hebrew) All food that is not kosher and hence forbidden by Jewish Law.

tucas: (Yiddish) The behind; the rear-end; the buttocks.

tzadik: (Yiddish and Hebrew) singular; a wise, religious/scholarly old man.

tzadik godol: (Yiddish and Hebrew) A very wise religious scholarly man, one who towers above all others.

tzadikim: (Yiddish and Hebrew) plural form. Wise, religious/scholarly old men.

tzedakah: (Yiddish and Hebrew) A righteous deed; also the giving of charity.

tzizis: (Yiddish and Hebrew) The fringes at the corner of the prayer shawl traditionally worn by Jewish men. The fringes contain 613 knots in all, each knot representing a seperate *mitzvot,* or commandment from the *Torah.*

yarmulke: (Yiddish) Skull cap worn by Orthodox Jewish men to show God their constant respect.

Yerushalayim: (Hebrew) Jerusalem.

Yeshiva: (Yiddish) Jewish day school originating in Eastern Europe for religious males to study the *Torah* and learn the holy language, Hebrew.

"yisgadal, viyiskadash, sh'mai rabo": (Aramaic) The Kaddish, Jewish prayer for the dead which affirms life, never mentions death itself.

Yitzhak: (Yiddish and Hebrew) A man's name from the Hebrew word meaning "to laugh."

Zayde: (Yiddish) Grandfather.

Writer, cultural activist, and performance artist, Jyl Lynn Felman has read her work throughout the US, Canada and England. She has performed in *Eye to Eye: Telling Stories, Breaking Boundaries, African American and Jewish American Women.* Her one-act play *Voices* was selected for the reading series at the 2nd International Women Playwrights Festival in Toronto, Canada and produced by the Evergreen Theater Festival. She is also an attorney, and lectures widely on racism, anit-Semitism, and homophobia.

   She received her MFA in fiction from the University of Massachusetts in Amherst where she was awarded a writing fellowship and has been a writer in residence at the Berkshire Forum. She is an award-winning short story writer whose work appears in over twenty newspapers, literary journals and anthologies. Her work can be found in *The Tribe of Dina, Word of Mouth, Loss Of The Ground-Note, Speaking For Ourselves,* and journals such as *Tikkun, Bridges, Lambda Book Report, Sojourner,* and *The National Women's Studies Journal.*

photo: Jean Weisinger

aunt lute books

is a multicultural women's press that has been committed to publishing high quality, culturally diverse literature since 1982. In 1990, the Aunt Lute Foundation was formed as a non-profit corporation to publish and distribute books that reflect the complex truths of women's lives and the possibilities for personal and social change. We seek work that explores the specificities of the very different histories from which we come, and that examines the intersections between the borders we all inhabit.

Please write or phone for a free catalogue of our other books or if you wish to be on our mailing list for future titles. You may buy books directly from us by phoning in a credit card order or mailing a check with the catalogue order form.

Aunt Lute Books
P.O. Box 410687
San Francisco, CA 94141
(415) 558-8116